NERVE DAMAGE

NERVE DAMAGE

Annakeara Stinson

SCRIBNER

London · New York · Amsterdam/Antwerp · Sydney/Melbourne · Toronto · New Delhi

First published in the United States by Alfred A. Knopf,
a division of Penguin Random House LLC, 2026

First published in Great Britain by Scribner, an imprint of
Simon & Schuster UK Ltd, 2026

1 3 5 7 9 10 8 6 4 2

Simon & Schuster UK Ltd, 7th Floor,
199 Bishopsgate, London, EC2M 3TY

Simon & Schuster Australia, Sydney
Simon & Schuster India, New Delhi

www.simonandschuster.co.uk
www.simonandschuster.com.au
www.simonandschuster.co.in

A CIP catalogue record for this book
is available from the British Library

Hardback ISBN: 978-1-3985-5645-4
eBook ISBN: 978-1-3985-5646-1
eAudio ISBN:

The authorised representative in the EEA is Simon & Schuster Netherlands BV,
Herculesplein 96, 3584 AA Utrecht, Netherlands. info@simonandschuster.nl

Printed and Bound in the UK using 100% Renewable Electricity
at CPI Group (UK) Ltd

For my mom

Afraid! Of whom am I afraid?

—EMILY DICKINSON

NERVE DAMAGE

1

It's the day before Halloween, and I've agreed to go to a concert at a venue called Afterlife with Bunny and this insufferable guy she's been dating. They go inside to get us drinks, and I stay back for some air at a picnic table on the floodlit concrete terrace where people smoke and drink on scattered classroom chairs and yard furniture. I've never been here but I know what kind of place it is since there are no classic costumes in sight—too cool for me to feel at ease. No bloody brides, no celebrity couples, no Scream masks. In fact, it's possible most people aren't wearing costumes, but who knows? It's as though aliens came down to Earth and were asked to dress a crowd of trendy youths. It's all sheepskin coats, flood-leg denim, latex bra tops, safety vests, gym shorts, shellacked hair, candy-stink vapes. I've perched atop a picnic table, and a girl comes over in a floor-length Lakers jersey, with impressive greenscale eye makeup and neon kitten heels. She crouches to look under the tables and asks if I've seen a phone. I haven't, but since this girl is clutching actual cigarettes, I ask for one. She hands one over—a menthol slim—without making eye contact and anxiously continues to search.

"Is it gauche and geriatric of me to ask if you're wearing a costume?" I say as somehow, by grace, I find matches in my jacket.

"Sorry?" She snaps to attention and gives an inscrutable

once-over to my black pants and nondescript black leather trench.

"Is that a costume?" I try again, gesturing toward the jersey dress. She leaves without answering as I fail to light the first match.

Inside the venue—a windowless black box with a two-foot-tall stage and a back bar—is an all-male free jazz trio called Digital Seizing. They are shirtless. I find Bunny and her new "situation," Chris, across the crowd. He bobs to the beat in deep concentration. Bunny's sister Nicole and I call Chris "Crust" because he owns a Cybertruck and works in the "explosive intersection of crypto and AI." At Afterlife, in his pristine white collar and Rolex, he looks like a stockbroker who got lost but refuses to admit the mistake. Bunny catches me laughing to myself, intuitively knows it's at Crust's expense, and gives me a look. It's like she can read my mind. She turns, grabs his jaw, and kisses him, proving something like a point, and the sight makes my gut lurch. It makes me glad I don't date.

That said, I admire Bunny because she's nothing like me. I am withered by life's blows, a hermit. She's resilient and action oriented, despite any hardship she's encountered. She was a golden tan, colicky Colombian baby adopted by cold WASPs who loved her conditionally—entertainment lawyers who provided her with high-thread-count sheets and expensive extracurriculars but wouldn't let her, for example, date, wear sportswear, or listen to Lauryn Hill. She joyfully rebelled instead of taking it personally. When Bunny was a freshman in high school she had a Lolita-esque relationship with an unhinged fifty-something female theater teacher. A few years ago, she had a lover die of a fentanyl overdose in her actual arms. Yet, she dates constantly and somewhat suspiciously or miraculously falls in love within six months of each previous longish-term relationship. She's an ideological bohemian, an actress, and doesn't like to be alone in that way, she tells me, what's the point? The little bits of people you get to learn about when you wake up with them, watch TV together, suck them off in a car. It's too rich! And because she's my best—leaning toward only—friend, I find myself enduring bits of all these people by proxy, much more than I'd like.

Projected in the background behind where Bunny and Crust stand is a scene from a French film—a pale young man is sucking a plump woman's nipples as she holds him like a baby. I go to the corner water station, a little inlet in the wall that's mosaicked in large, jagged pieces of broken mirror. Next to me is a wasted girl dressed up like a circus clown, red nose and all. I almost give thanks for her directness. I move aside and the two of us rapidly fill and refill our tiny triangular cups of cold water. Now that I'm defensively hydrated, I need a real shot.

I turn toward the bar and stop short. My skin becomes goose-flesh, my mind goes static. *No.* But yes. There sits P.T. on a stool. Chatting with the bartender. I don't have my glasses and it's dark, so it's possible my eyes are tricking me, maybe I've forgotten what he really looks like, maybe that water was doused with acid. It's too on the nose that I see him today of all days.

But there he is, I swear to god. P.T. has his elbow on the bar, cheek in hand, and he's flirting with a curly-haired, redheaded, beautiful bartender. Nary a care has he. I go to therapy twice a week and have the sexual prowess of unleavened bread—he's here, in my new city, flirting. A candle flickers below his face. He's lost some weight; his hair is even longer, still bountiful, dark gold, and held back in part by invisible and poorly placed bobby pins. Still, those sunken, practically black eyes. He's wearing a brown suede bomber jacket. I watch him talk to the woman. She puts her forearms down on the bar and leans in, her neck cranes up, her expression too wide open. Freckled and dare I say zaftig, in the process of being hypnotized by his bizarre charm. That's me I'm looking at, in one way or another. It's me and P.T., it's P.T. and who knows how many more random women in bars and bodega lines. That's P.T. and the woman who finally broke us. Lisa from Tinder. I get a sudden and obtrusive vision of P.T. giving all three of us orgasms at once: me on a hand, Lisa on his face, the bartender on, well.

This is not how I imagined a chance encounter. I imagined a lethal threat—he'd crawl through my apartment window in one of the dresses I left at his place, or pop out of a trash can with an AK-47. Perhaps one day he would walk into my coffee place and stab me before stabbing himself. I should probably leave, that seems like the best possible idea, but I can't move. As far as I know, he hasn't seen me. He was never very perceptive, has poor vision himself. From the looks of things, he's halfway through some dark liquor drink. Likely not his first.

I dig my nails into my palms, strain my eyes toward him, but P.T.—or P.T.'s simulacrum—is leaned away from me now, preventing a longer look at his face. I see him blow out the candle and pour the wax on his hand, and then a little on hers as she shrieks in laughter. It's him. It has to be him.

Finally, I recoup enough wind to run over to Bunny and Crust. Bunny looks at my face, which must appear palsied, then snaps her fingers at me.

"Uh, babe? You good?"

I open then close my mouth. I'm not interested in having Bunny confront P.T. or explaining my dark past to Crust.

"Getting a migraine," I say. "Very nauseous."

"Oh god, you want some Advil? I have a ton . . ."

"No! I think I have some here!" I pretend to start searching in my purse but clumsily I spill the contents and out come my keys, sunglasses, a peppermint Lip Smacker, a parking ticket, prescription sleeping pills, and a pack of grape Hi-Chews.

"You want me to bring you home?" Crust asks when I pop back up from the floor, now overheating.

"I'll do an Uber!" I smile weakly, give Bunny a kiss on the cheek, and slip out the side door. Not before taking another small peek in P.T.'s direction, my sunglasses on and the collar of my coat popped. But this time, he looks up. Directly at me. He smiles.

When I get back to my apartment, there's an envelope taped to my door. It contains two used Q-tips. Immediate gag reflex. I saw it before I left and thought it was a note from the building manager. I've had bizarre things left at my door multiple times this month. A pair of dirty socks, a wet newspaper, *The Book of Miracles.* Those seemed like potential mistakes. The people in this deteriorating art deco four-story are oddballs, East Hollywood is no man's land. The guy who lives across the hall from me has never looked me in the eye, wears nightgowns, and has hair down to his ass. The woman next to him has nine snakes.

There's a couple down the hall from me on the first floor I call the Screaming Birds, as they fight with disturbing constancy and have a nervous-sounding parakeet. I have borne witness to more than one 5150 in this building. I got the place when I moved out here pretty broke, having used the last of my money on a lawyer. I have a good job, but I'm still here nevertheless, comforted by the company of a white noise machine and a dead bolt. After tonight, after seeing P.T., I have a new theory about the origin of these seemingly disconnected items. He is an artist, after all, of the attempted avant-garde. He loves impossible symbolism.

After scrubbing my hands, I pace for a while. I turn on some classical music and all my lamps. I light a stick of palo santo. I'm wired and I really don't want to think about P.T., so I'll do some work instead. I get my laptop out, get in bed, arrange my down quilt tightly around my legs, and fluff my myriad of pillows. This is where I belong and where I spend much of my time. I'm a package designer for an adult toy company called MaidenToyage—this week's task is making insignias for butt plugs and the holiday-flavored organic lubes. It will clear my head to work. So much of his harassment was digital, so if I put any energy in that direction, I fear it will reconnect us, link us spiritually. That somehow he will know. I haven't checked his socials or even googled him since the moment I left him. I can't start now, it will lead me straight to the void.

Around 4 a.m. I click on his X account (@bloodblister00). It's nothing revelatory, betrays no place of residence. Retweets of self-proclaimed leftist internet bros. Long threads about closing Rikers and corrupt media outlets—convoluted and manic, but I'll admit, well argued. Links to sites where he's published art or political criticism in obscure online zines and alt-culture blogs. I find a few published poems.

LOVE IS A WIRECUTTER

desire is a sad knife, limbs jamming about
rotten old fruits too formidable to destroy
drips of inner skin fused with slick rock
lick the dead tissue that resists light
nearly alive, zen by way of electrocution

GIVETH, TAKETH AWAY

do I want to watch her bleed
the answer is yes
the question is
how do I know
it's blood

I read them over and over again. The second one, of course, causes acute pangs of terror. I imagine it's me he wants to watch bleed. I look through his Instagram pictures next—he hasn't posted in almost a year. Before that it's "found art" on city walks, pictures of his shadow, or art-art, like a Giacometti at the Met. His last post is a picture taken from behind—a young child in a red sweatsuit, looking intently at something in a puddle on the street. The damp armpits of my cotton pajamas stick to my skin. I'm sucked into his vortex. Even through the internet his power seeps in like a scentless, sightless poison. My body conjures up the same physical sensations of dread I had at the end of my time in New York, the desire to morph into something else, for my skin to melt, to perhaps be swallowed by my warm bed, never to be seen by another living being. My life in LA isn't wildly social, by any means, but I haven't been concerned about walking down a street or into a restaurant. Or I wasn't until tonight.

I'm still looking for P.T. evidence when my mother calls me at 8 a.m. to tell me she and Mitch are getting married. It's almost funny, my mother's celebratory announcement arriving as I'm mentally hurtling backward to my worst relationship, in bed with a bowl of cold spaghetti. Her love life has always been more active than mine. Like Bunny, her lust for intimacy has never been dampened by her previous failures.

"He asked and I said yes!" she screams when I pick up, and somewhere in the background, Mitch adds, "She said yes!"

Mitch is by no means Mom's second time at the bridal rodeo. But it's her first local find in upstate New York since moving there many years ago. Minus my dad, the other husbands have been out-of-state gentlemen from Match.com. Mitch owns the lumberyard. Her friend Sue set them up. At first she was completely disinterested—a man who "worked in wood" she "could only assume" was "simple." But she started seeing him differently, she told me, a few months after their first meeting. He came to each date with flowers, didn't kiss her right away, and always paid for their dinner with crisp hundreds. Now they live together in a timber-frame house he built for her. A far cry from the flat-roofed modular she settled us into when I was a child.

"Of course he has that bum hip, so he couldn't kneel," she says with a sigh, describing the special moment at their favorite restaurant, Pagliacci's. I can hear her pop the cork of a bottle of wine and begin to pour. It's 11 a.m. on the East Coast.

"I thought you said you were too old for marriage," I say, putting her on speakerphone so I can continue looking at P.T.'s tagged photos. I click on to the profile of a guy with a septum piercing (@lowlvlcrown) sitting across from him at a Korean restaurant (discomfiting since there are many in LA, not so many in New York), then decide to look at the profile of everyone tagged on @lowlvlcrown's whole grid, eventually landing me knee-deep in the profile of @lowlvlcrown's mother, @donna_dewell54, chiropractor and "Airedale guardian" living in Bangor, Maine. There's no reasoning to my research at this point. Yet, I feel a thorough combing of everything he's attached to online, and everything that everything he's attached to is attached to, has to lead to information. There has to be a way to find out where he is.

"Too old for marriage? I wouldn't have called myself old, Clarice." My mother teeters on the edge of whining. I can see her gently brushing away strands of her hair, eyes closing, fluttering, tics she has when she is feeling offended.

"Maybe you said 'evolved'?" I consider telling her about P.T. in hopes she will assure me I certainly imagined it, that I have always been a girl with a toe or two on the ground and a brain in the clouds, that it is my inventive spirit getting the best of me. But I know she would think I was trying to one-up her.

She would get angry or dramatically frightened, make me talk to Mitch about purchasing a handgun as she wept loudly in the background, and request that I move closer to home. Not that we saw each other much when I lived in New York. The truth is, I would say to her, that if he lives here, there's nothing I can do about it. As of about a month ago—the restraining order has run its course. He could be my fucking neighbor if he wanted. I would tell her that, and know that it's true, and I'd be scared, and she wouldn't be able to comfort me.

"I was thinking you and your brother could officiate the ceremony, though I haven't mentioned it to Damian yet . . ." Mom clears her throat. "Something medium-sized. Friends, family, the guys from Mitch's lumberyard."

"You're having an actual wedding?"

I'm not upset about the marriage. Mitch will be my fourth dad, and while I suspect he's involved in a relatively mild-mannered but still questionable redneck mob, he thinks my mom is a gift from the angels who crafted the symptoms of her personality disorder simply to make him chuckle. He's also pretty funny and sends me greeting cards with cash at random.

Events with my mother are never easy, and they bring up reminders of her previous matrimonies. We lived in poorly insulated subsidized artist housing in Chelsea until I was twelve—then my mom left my dad and brought us, by cover of night, to live upstate. Soon accompanied by Ken, a young Polish video game designer, who came up from Delaware to become her second husband based on a purely online long-distance relationship. A man who punched me in the face after the rehearsal dinner because I called him a perverted little bitch. Not stellar behavior on my part, but I was drunk on bubbly and he had told me my dress would look nicer if it was taken in tighter at the bust. My mom screamed as Damian peeled Ken's body off mine—Ken, who was spitting and yelling that I should be put in my place. Still, the next evening at the ceremony I recited Walt Whitman's "Fast Anchor'd, Eternal, O Love," wearing sunglasses, clutching a bouquet of thistle and dried lavender. My thoughts on her boyfriends felt relatively insignificant from then on. It got worse with the next husband—an orthorexic cokehead engineer named Hugh she married when I was in high school. My anguished teen plan was to get him to make a pass at me, then I'd tell my mother so she would leave his ass with a nice settlement. Instead of waiting for him to come to me, I went out to his garage office one night and asked if he could teach me to give blow jobs. I'd had a few secret wine coolers. Maybe to his credit, there was a very pregnant pause before he unzipped his pants. I didn't do it, thank god. I was shocked it worked, so I pivoted by asking him to take sexy pictures of me for a fake internet boyfriend instead. I should have left but there I stood in my little white bra from Macy's while he pulled out a digital camera. I never told my mother any of this. I deleted the pictures and contemplated death for months on end. I figured I would go to an out-of-state college at least five hours away by plane. But he and my mother divorced not long after that incident, when he left her for a much, much older woman with whom he had secretly started a camgirl website. They met in a chatroom for people who like big-bush porn. My mother was so devastated she asked for nothing in the divorce, and we were broke again.

"What's wrong with celebrating the love of a good man?" she whispers to me. I can hear her padding down the hall, then closing a door.

"Nothing." I sigh, now looking through all of P.T.'s followers. Not many, 325. It won't take that long to comb through every public profile to see if there are untagged photos of him, or if he's left any telling comments on their posts.

"After what I've been through with some of these losers?" Mom says in response to my loaded quiet. I hear her turn on the TV and immediately lower the volume to a mumble.

"Congratulations, Ma."

"Don't call me that, Clarice. It sounds trashy." Her tone changes from annoyed to surrendering. The last time we spoke she told me not to make so many jokes, it made me seem masculine. "Also, I wanted to ask, have you spoken to your father?"

"What? No. I never talk to him. Why?"

"Oh, I just . . . It's not my business, Clarice. Damian was saying he really hasn't been doing well."

"When has he ever done well?" I asked. Some years ago now my father had an addiction-related aneurysm that left him without control of his legs or arms and unable to speak. A variety of his organs didn't seem to take the shock well. It disturbed me deeply, we were all sure he was going to die. We weren't in touch at that point, but I broke no-contact and sent kind voice notes for his girlfriend to play for him in the hospital. I asked to be added to the email chain where she sent daily updates reporting his blood pressure and level of consciousness. I did daily meditations, including one entitled "How to Help a Loved One Exit the Mortal Coil." Then—he bounced back. He uses a wheelchair and is mostly paralyzed, but he can talk again. I felt betrayed by myself that I'd gotten so emotionally involved. This foul-mouthed vampire who sent the occasional stuffed animal in lieu of child support had wriggled his way back into my heart, filling it with sympathy. But he rose again, determined to watch a few more hours of TV, rail painkillers, and verbally abuse his new home nurse. Now we don't talk at all, but Damian keeps in sporadic contact with him. Apparently, he's as pissed off as ever, and every eighteen months or so he's dying again.

"Oh, my faux pas, *forgive me* for asking about him. We were only together for fifteen years. Honestly, what I'm most concerned with right now is how soon Mitch and I want to have the ceremony. I'm feeling sort of puffy . . ."

"You're beautiful, Mom." Which is true. So was my dad,

long ago. They were both New York theater people and my mom modeled for extra money. As Bunny once said, "They might be insane, but at least they're good-looking!" Genes that seem to have skipped a generation, as Damian and I have always read as slightly haunted.

"I know, Clarice, but it's about what one feels internally."

"Gotta de-puff the soul," I say with a laugh that gets strangled, because I find what I'm looking for. A picture of P.T. in California. I've ended up on the account of his cousin Daniel, a professional deadbeat who lives in Seattle, and in Dan's tagged photos, there he is with P.T. Sitting on the grass in Griffith Park, holding a Tecate. I can see the orb of the observatory behind him. P.T. is looking down at his feet, pulling up grass. He never liked getting his picture taken—he's awkward around most people and he thinks because his eyes are so dark, pictures make him look evil. He's not wrong. He had a tradition of visiting Daniel every year, so maybe they came down to LA this time. But he's wearing a brown bomber, just like the P.T. I saw talking to the bartender.

"Mom, I gotta jet. I'm going trick-or-treating with Bunny and her nieces," I say, interrupting a tangent I dissociated from about retinol and placing cold spoons under her eyes.

"Well, happy Halloween!" she sings into a sip of wine.

2

There was something off about his smile. Perhaps because his teeth were so small he had to stretch his lips tall and wide to prove his mouth wasn't a black hole. It seems dumb and even cruel that I saw him again on the night before Halloween. Once my favorite holiday, and now, perpetually, the day I left him three years ago. The strongest memories of P.T. arrive yearly along with piles of pumpkin-shaped Snickers, Jason masks at CVS, and the massive, pointedly metaphorical skeletons Angelenos love to have stationed on their porches. October brings a crawling anxiety, often a cold or the flu, then thoughts of him, dreams. Halloween is every crevice of his face, his smell, our holidays together, our sex, the threats he made long after the initial breakup. Blunt grief and fear and sometimes relief that I got out. But this year has felt different, more potent. Perhaps I prophesied this; for about a month now I've been dreaming about him—these mundane scenarios where I'm washing dishes or lying in bed and get the uneasy feeling he's lurking in a corner, watching. It feels like he astral-projected himself into my dreams, like it's intentional. A fail-safe way to stay in my life without consent.

The day I left, P.T. and I were supposed to go to my office Halloween party at a roller rink, costumed as a pair of dice. As usual when I stayed over at his place, we were inert, rotting the day away. P.T. lay on his bed looking at his phone, his die costume deflated in a pile next to him, three huge dots facing up.

I had on my bra, black tights, white face paint, really making an effort to get dressed. I crawled up on P.T. at one point, after receiving a *Where are you? Boss George is SCHWASTED!!!!!!!* text from a coworker; straddled him; and started nipping at his neck a little, thinking it might call him to action. He playfully tried to dodge me by turning away his face from a kiss but started unbuckling his belt. I stopped, sat up, and placed my hands on my hips.

"Boner killer, but my vulva is fucking on fire," I said. I had felt physically uncomfortable during sex for about a month, and now the irritation got worse as I was grinding my hips in those tights against his groin. The pain was lingering. I had chosen to ignore it in favor of maintaining intimacy. But it was beginning to concern me.

"You think you gave me the clap?" I asked, cocking my head to the side, eyebrows up. I was joking, I remember that, but an expression erupted on his face—so surprised and timid. An instant blush, his ears practically folded down.

"What was that look?" I asked, my own face feeling as if it were about to fall off.

"What was what?" His eyes went dumb—it brought to mind a cow chewing cud. He tried to force a frown, but his mouth began to twitch.

"That look," I repeated as it dawned totally. "Did you sleep with someone?"

So odd, those moments when the truth finally rises, the world stills. For better or worse it really does set you free, particularly of the torture of second-guessing yourself. I was always suspicious of him, which he liked to point out frequently—but, then, he often acted suspiciously. Weird, sudden phone calls he'd take outside his apartment, disappearing for days at a time, not showing up to dates. Always some unassailable excuse. An issue his mother was having, his own spells of depression, a simple need for solitude and boundaries.

He rolled me off him, groaning.

"We fucked once, that's it," he said, standing up, not facing me. I knew it was more.

"Who was it?"

"A stranger."

I reached for a T-shirt that had been crumpled on the floor and used it, in vain, to wipe away some of my Halloween-spirit, graffiti-grade face paint. I noticed the shirt had previously been used as a jizz rag.

"How did you meet?" I asked, rapidly searching for a clean spot.

"How do you think?"

He walked out of the room into the kitchen and I followed him, arms now shot to the sky.

"A *bar*?"

"Tinder."

"You're on Tinder?" I yelled.

"I don't think so, anymore."

"What do you mean, *you don't think so*?" I placed my hands on my hips, then across my chest, then back on my hips.

"You know, Big Tech." He filled a glass with water and took a sip, just as I felt the strain of tears at my throat. "Nothing is ever gone."

I made him go through the event step by step. When it happened, he told me, we had been fighting again. It was the day he dropped me off at the airport to go to Montana for my uncle Tim's funeral, and, well, he thought I was lying. He thought I was off to fuck a college fling who was now an econ professor in Bozeman, he said, that Tim's death was a front.

"Oh, Tim is *dead*," I said, at the kitchen sink, once again attempting to scrub my dice face paint off, now with a sopping paper towel and cheap dish soap. The smell of dirty sponge engulfed me. "I read a Rumi poem at the memorial."

He went on. He downloaded the app—in grief, out of spite.

A beautiful woman had matched with him immediately. He could tell she was "intrigued" by how quickly she messaged him. He could tell by her aesthetic—"she had a Longchamp tote, unfortunate highlights"—that she wasn't someone he would ever take seriously. They decided to meet at a bar that night.

"And then what?" I asked, crumpling my body to sit down on the kitchen floor in one corner, across from him, as he sat in a chair at the dinky metal breakfast table, alert. "You met up and got drunk and what?"

"Lisa and I talked."

"About what?"

"Our childhoods. Extinction discourse. You."

"That's deranged, P.T."

"Not really *you*, Clarice. The idea of you. It was an erotic tactic."

"It was an erotic tactic," I sneered back at him.

"I told her you had never orgasmed before me." He looked down at his hands, sheepish.

"Are you for real?"

"She related, for what it's worth."

"And you told Lilah you could get her there?" Now my arms were crossed so tightly against my chest my breasts felt like they were bruising.

"Lisa. Yes, I said I could."

"And did you?"

He pressed his lips together, trying to hide his pride. I kicked the wall, letting out a bleat, really, and punched him hard on the upper arm as I ran past him, intending to go pack a suitcase. A task that would prove to take me many, many hours. "Ow, Clarice, come on, baby!" he yelled, and tramped after me.

Halloween fireworks went off in Prospect Park throughout the evening, right outside the window, as we continued to fight. Orange, white, purple, and blue, some of them in the bloated shape of a jack-o'-lantern, shattering through the air as I gulped and whimpered and cried, as I tackled him on the couch, as he flipped me and pinned me down, shook my shoulders, yelled. When I finally got the gumption to leave the apartment, I passed a sexpotted My Little Pony, a Michael Myers, a Charlie Chaplin. I was crazed and wet in the face, heaving my half-broken wheely suitcase down the side of the road. Toward freedom? He followed me. The streets were infested. Firecrackers, pops, explosions, smoke. Drunk people, good-looking, homely, sweating, en route somewhere. The trick-or-treaters were gone at this point, maybe a few errant tweens in half-costumes with pillowcases. Mostly adults looking to forget work, to fuck one another with masks on. The night of a thousand little fantasies. We fought loudly on a bench and eventually we were both so tired we went for wood-fired pizza at a pretty nice place. We went back to his apartment.

The doorbell rang at some point. He'd forgotten—a Polish couple from Airbnb were renting out his extra room for the week. Their first trip to the States. They were beautiful dirty-blondes with eyes just a little too blue. They looked like siblings. They had brought P.T. a thank-you present. Some tea. I sat grinding my teeth and giving him deadly stares when they weren't paying attention. Together the four of us enjoyed a fragrant, bitter jasmine.

A few days later I made P.T. meet me after my STD screening so he could bring some stuff I'd left at his house. He told me not to bring him any items he had left at my apartment, said I should just keep or burn them. We went to a tin-box diner on one of those winding lost streets in FiDi afterward. A part of Manhattan that gives off edge and end-of-the-world vibes. Constitutionally on the brink of rain, plus Wall Street. I had made an immediate gynecological appointment after the Lisa revelation. During our fight it came to light he'd read some "dark web blog pieces in high school" about health clinics collecting DNA for government testing. "Yes," he'd said, "I fucking fibbed about previous screenings."

I felt a sick sense of obligation to whomever he slept with next, and I planned for my results to be the next and last time I would contact him. I could tell when he arrived, with a plastic bag that held a single bedtime shirt and a hairbrush that wasn't mine, that he did not think this was the end. To be fair, I'd broken up with P.T. multiple times during the last half of our yearlong relationship and it never stuck, it didn't work, so he probably thought this was one of those times, theatrics.

But something broke open in me, some realization that I could choose not to be with him and that would be that. Usually, I'd get upset with him for something like lying about where he'd been or going off the grid, and by the end of the fight the problem became my rigidity, my subconsciously puritanical values. Perhaps there was some truth in that? Who was I to tell him where he was supposed to be, how frequently we were supposed to talk, that he shouldn't have a folder of raunchy pictures of his exes on his laptop entitled "posterititty"? You can't make *demands* of other people, he would tell me. You can't *transfer* the grief of your father's *abandonment* onto *me*, he would say. And then later, when we calmed down, after angrily fucking, he'd say, "But I can help you get through your pain."

Toward the middle and end of our relationship, I got more concerned with his moods. I stayed at his place in Lefferts Gardens as much as he'd let me, which meant I started witnessing his manic episodes. I told him it made me nervous when he would randomly quit his already very part-time jobs, or that I thought it was a bad idea for him to sell all his kitchen supplies and his only computer on Craigslist when he needed cash. That it didn't seem, to me, like a "creative retreat" when he woke up coked out in the Rockaways.

At the diner, after my doctor's appointment, P.T. and I got fries and orange juice and he tried to explain himself to me one more time, with a little more feeling. He didn't realize how much he loved me until he slept with someone else, he said. And I should understand that in part it was my neediness in our relationship that had caused him to stray. He had never been with someone he could really trust before, he said, and that made him want to test my loyalty. I could sense an underlying smugness; he thought I'd cave. Usually, I was drawn to audacity. It signaled an inaccessibility, emotionally speaking, a challenge to which my wanting soul was programmed to rise. He told me sorry again and again while we sat there, sipping. I told him that while it was true that I was inherently jealous, our breakup wasn't really about that. He asked, unconvinced, what it was about.

"We aren't good for each other. At all."

He raised an eyebrow at me. Chewed some ice. "Well, I disagree. And punishing me so harshly for one mistake is really juvenile behavior."

Outside our window stood a mortally exhausted old man beholding the sky as it broke. Rain increased in volume exponentially as the seconds passed. I wondered why the man was wearing an ankle-length raincoat if he was just going to let himself get soaked. I also thought, *I feel you, brother.* P.T. reached over to my cheek and wiped off a crumb I doubt was even there. I told him I had to meet someone. He asked me to split the bill.

"Is Maxine telling you we should break up?" P.T. asked as we waited for the rain to soften under the diner awning, then walked to his train stop on the nearby corner. I blew a subdued raspberry. Maxine was my Craigslist roommate turned pretty-much-friend, a woman nearly ten years older than me who ran a design firm from the living room—she built brand identity for other Black-owned businesses. She rented me my room for extra cash, she said, even though she seemed to do very well. It was affordable and more beautiful than any place I'd ever lived, so I cleaned the common spaces a lot and spent most of my time in my room. I didn't understand why she'd want a roommate until one night, after some wine, she told me that she lost her partner to colon cancer a few years before I moved in. Her high school sweetheart. He had inherited the apartment, paid off, from his grandma and then he left it to Maxine. My presence was more of a loneliness thing than a money thing, but she also didn't want a new best friend. She thought that wouldn't be a problem with me. I thought she was great.

From the get-go, Maxine said P.T. seemed like a "disturbed bookworm with a lethal ego" after he came to our Bed-Stuy apartment for dinner and started describing Lacanian analysis to her, unsolicited, as she passed through the kitchen. Even then I believed her assessment more than I didn't—but something about him enchanted me. I didn't know how he felt about me at all, or what he did when we weren't together. That hooked me. But P.T. could tell Maxine didn't buy what he was selling, clear in the deadened expression she wore each time he spoke. Maxine said "shocker" when I told her about P.T. fucking around. She told me to block his ass. Maxine thought I shouldn't even meet up with P.T. that day. She said the closer I got to him, the closer I was to the danger of his bullshit.

"Maxine is not *not* saying that," I told P.T., who was looking down at his phone and rapid-fire texting. Must have been Lisa from Tinder.

"What a nosy bitch," he said, looking up, shaking his head. "I'm sure you painted yourself as an angel, right? Didn't mention how you make me feel guilty all the time?"

"Sure."

"How about I call you in a week or so? Reassess."

"I'm serious, P.T., I don't want to talk."

“Listen, I told you, I needed a little time to realize you were the one.”

“And as I told you, I’m done.”

“Okay, right, have it your way, I don’t need you either.” He exhaled and leaned in for a kiss, which I evaded. It was those quick shifts in mood that reminded me I was making the right decision.

“So, it’s like that?” he asked. I gave him the finger and he laughed with his mouth open. I glared at the coyote tattoo on his hand to avoid direct eye contact. He blew me a kiss and started walking backward toward the subway, only turning away when he reached the top of the stairs.

That hideous tattoo was the first thing I noticed about him. I thought it was cool. Cool enough to accept a pale yellow pill from him on the dance floor at a party of a girl I knew from college. I turned around and there he was, flopping his wild flow of hair back with that canine-inked hand, in a button-down that pulled at the chest. Gleaming, obsidian eyes. We moved together and eventually he handed me that pill. I asked what it was about twenty minutes after I swallowed, when I started feeling in love with myself, fellow partygoers, the floor, fingers as a concept. He mumbled something in my ear.

“Wait, *what*?” I asked, nearly screaming, as my bones left my body and I became simple limbs of pumping, happy blood.

“It’s angel dust,” he said, grabbing me by the waist and pulling me in toward him. “It rules.” The lights met the sweat on his neck and glimmered, swirled into rainbow colors, the way they move in gasoline. I stuck out my tongue and licked. He licked me back. I noticed how his eyes lost focus before he kissed me, goofy and vulnerable in a way that seemed almost brave. There was no shame in his kiss, that was my first thought when our mouths hit, he really did it for pleasure. And I felt real pleasure, too, the soft heat of his mouth enveloping to the point where I lost track of myself in him, my perception started cracking into something new, into the sense that my body was a whole day at once, my stomach dusk arriving, my lungs night, my skull a young dawn, and all of me breathing, breathing, breathing.

Then of course I woke up from a blackout sitting outside my building, smelling like rancid meat. My only concern was that the man I danced with the night before, whose name I didn't know, whose phone number was written in Sharpie on my forearm, must be made my husband. We started dating.

I got a call from an NP the following week with my results from the test that day.

"No STDs, and you didn't even come back positive for vaginosis or a UTI," she told me.

"Okay, so you're saying my crotch is burning for no reason?" I asked.

"Your vulva is trying to tell you something."

"Like I was in the wrong relationship?"

She let out a long sigh; it sounded weighted. "Or the wrong kind of underwear."

P.T. texted me a few days later that he was *clean, too, baby*. I didn't respond. The next day he called me five times. I didn't pick up. He left me minutes-long voice messages, all starting with: *I know we're not talking*. It was unusual, this persistence. He had never done this before. Usually he was hard to keep track of, and he was never a repeat caller to anyone unless he was in a fight with a customer service person, his landlord, or the under-the-radar Airbnb subletters who left his extra room unclean, people whom he took discomfiting pleasure in tormenting. Perhaps he never did this to me because I had never succeeded in wronging him, I was always the one who felt hurt, who wanted. Wanted him to be affectionate, findable, doting. Wanted him to love me more than his exes, more than his mother, more than the women we passed on the street. Panic was a feeling that never left my body the whole time we were together, as was longing. The longing had gone, and perhaps he could feel that. Now he was the one who felt unwanted, and it seemed to unsettle him enough to make him hungry for me. The next day I woke to a text from him, something he sent at three in the morning.

You like this, don't you, you sick little bitch, he wrote, and sent me a short video of himself masturbating. An act of observation I used to truly enjoy.

P.T. Stop. Contacting. Me. We have broken up.

He sent back a thumbs-up emoji, then he wrote, *I fucked myself thinking about you.* I still rubbed off to the video before deleting it, felt self-loathing and pervy afterward. In a way, it was the last time we had sex. The last time I had sex at all, really.

3

He sent actual mail, after I stopped responding to his texts and calls. "Love letters," which were simply written-out versions of the same conversation we'd had ten times before I stopped talking to him:

> *. . . I had been betrayed before. I believed you were intending to cheat on me to provoke jealousy, so yes, I had intercourse with a useless stranger. I am asking you with a bleeding heart to respond to my wishes and speak to me once again. My love for you has become boundless. I want you to know how I feel about you, how deeply my love for you runs. I was distant to you in the past, sometimes dismissive. But it was the fault of unethical previous unions. From now on, my modus operandi is chivalry, loyalty, transparency.*

He numbered the letters and promised he'd write 365 of them, to signify the time we spent together. When the first four got no response from me, he sent indignant emails asking for his stuff back, which I had thrown out when he told me to. ("I need my shit back. My Miles Davis record and my copy of *The Master and Margarita*. Probably some clothes. You're being awful.")

Then more of the same letters came again, day after day. Rapid-fire. He got up to twelve physical letters before he started using email again, sent from a small variety of addresses: Peeteeplease@gmail.com, PTphonehome@gmail.com, mistakenman@gmail.com. Then a made-up dermatologist's office (Dr. Conor Bogsworth, MD), then a fake business (BKBeeswaxcandles).

Every other day I'd get NO ID calls that I didn't pick up. A notice he wanted to connect on LinkedIn, a request to refriend him on Facebook, and vague "hello" messages from Instagram accounts that had no friends or followers. These would roll in over the span of a few hours. You don't realize how free you are just walking around living life until you aren't anymore, until you're always expecting something.

Maxine was the only one around at the time. Damian, my mom, and I didn't often express earnest feelings with one another. Bunny was already back in LA. We had lived in New York together since college, but by the time we were twenty-six her dad had died and her mom wasn't far behind—so she wanted to be home near her sister. She was the social one, the intimate one; I just had casual friends and coworkers. Maxine said P.T. was really starting to concern her. Not a doctor, she diagnosed him as bipolar and recounted that her cousin had a stalker she met on Hinge who tried to poison her dog. She told me to block every account and number on everything—my phone, Instagram, Facebook, Twitter. Make my LinkedIn private. So I did. She told me that the next time he contacted me, it was time to make a police report. I told her that was not necessary.

"You realize what's happening right now is very much classified as warning signs, right? Harassment?"

I assured her that in time, he'd get the picture.

As if on cue, twenty minutes later, an email plopped into my inbox from yet another strange address.

Clarice, please. I need you to listen to me. My love for you has truly solidified since our break. I admire the passion with which you are expressing your anger. It shows a woman who loves herself. And I hope, a woman who loves me. I'm not going anywhere.

It went on, and beneath his signature (*Only Love & Light, P.T.*) was a link to a YouTube video of Dido's "White Flag."

Days later, he began sending emails and Facebook messages to family or friends of mine he'd only met once or twice, telling them he was worried that I had borderline personality disorder. Bunny got one, as did her sister, Nicole, as did my brother, Damian, as did Merce, a guy I used to cater-waiter with in my early twenties—we had run into him at a bar once early on in our relationship and had gotten a few drinks together. P.T. told them of my purported symptoms: I made him a villain, I had iced him out, I was frequently unreasonable, emotionally volatile. He placed links to mental health organizations below his signature. He told them to help me. I got more emails, still, sometimes with an original song attached or a poem. I forwarded them all to Maxine, who emailed back versions of the same thing: *Clarice! THIS IS NOT A DRILL! This guy is a level 10 psycho! BLOCK HIM AGAIN.*

One night, just after midnight, he called me on a Google phone number, and when I picked up, he said my name. I hung up immediately. I slept with the light on. In the morning I woke to yet another long email from a new account—he wanted me to know that he wasn't desperate to talk, he only called from the Google phone in order to see if his number had been blocked. He wanted to be on good terms, and we needed to be adults about this. Also he wanted his shit back.

At that point, I asked Damian to call P.T. and tell him to leave me alone. Damian is a reserved, jacked gay in the Air National Guard whom P.T. found intimidating, so I figured his words might land. I hadn't mentioned anything to Damian about P.T.'s strange behavior until he got that email, so I had to come out with all of it. I surprised myself by crying so hard when I called him I had to hang up and text him. I sat in my closet weeping on a pile of my shoes, leaning against my hamper, thumbing away. *P.T. has been harassing me, all these calls and emails, he won't stop. He's starting to freak me out. I'm not answering any of them, I told him multiple times to leave me alone.* Damian told me that P.T. gave him the willies when they met, so his behavior, while disturbing, didn't surprise him.

wish u told me u disliked him earlier

Oh, please. You would have rushed to a chapel!

I value ur POV

Not a judgment but you sometimes cling to these sweaty Rasputin men.

There's not much an outsider can do.

I thought I loved him.

Indeed, that much was clear.

Lol "not a judgment"

Damian called him and told him to please stay away from me, and to stop reaching out to me in any form. Breakups are hard, but this was not okay. He was violating my boundaries, he was starting to scare me. Apparently P.T. muttered, "Okay," and hung up fast.

P.T. was quiet for over a week after Damian called him. I thought I was in the clear. It was well into December at that point. Freezing and depressing in New York City. Then one day, a junior graphic designer awkwardly approached my desk at work.

"Clarice, I think your boyfriend is outside. Across the street?" he kindly whispered so no one would hear. He no doubt recognized P.T. from the company barbecue. P.T. came as my date and ate seven loaded hot dogs—it left a lasting impression on people. "He was just sort of standing there, staring over here. In front of the crepe place. I said hi but that seemed to make him, maybe, upset?"

I put my head in my hands. "I'm single now," I said as I felt a brick land in my chest. I left work two hours late that day. He was gone by the time I left.

That night, Bunny—who only met P.T. once—told me she'd gotten another Facebook message from him, telling her that he saw one of my coworkers see him outside of my workplace, and he didn't want me to think he was over that way because of me.

He said he was on 10th "shopping"

I guess it's possible?

Yes, I'm sure he was getting a nice pair of
leather pants at Comme des Garcons

there's other stores.

Anthropologie

I shouldn't respond, right? You should just
go to the police?

In the next few weeks came the gifts. I got flowers at my desk at work. "Did you make up?" asked the junior graphic designer. At home, more flowers. A jumbo cookie. I received a gift certificate for an "ancestral release massage" sent from a local spa from an anonymous donor. Then a ticket to a Butoh performance with a handwritten note:

I'll be waiting on the stairs at BAM before the show. The day after Christmas. Let art heal us.

When I didn't show up at the performance, I got another email. This time from a "Linda MacLean."

It's P.T., not Linda MacLean. You're being cruel, Clarice. You are enjoying it. What will it take for you to relinquish this imbalanced control and become my partner again? My fight is not over. I can't have you ruin me in this way. I can't sleep, I can't eat, I'm rapidly losing weight, and I am constantly crying. You are cruel. At this time of year no less.

When he wrote anything longer than a text, it tended to be a little formal and dramatic, but these emails seemed particularly departed from reality. I knew for a fact he was eating because I got multiple email receipts from our once-joint Seamless account. He'd never been remotely insistent about the future of our relationship when we were in it. This was a guy who gave me a sheet of stickers he found on the sidewalk for Valentine's Day after I gave him a homemade patchwork pillow and *The Selected Letters of John Keats*. A guy who told me I didn't have a certain je ne sais quoi that "his women usually have." The guy who simply had to share that he wasn't crazy about the color of the Agent Provocateur set I spent 450 bucks on. Something I bought after he'd asked, in disgust, if I'd gotten my underwear at Duane Reade.

And, then, finally, eventually, he showed up again. One

morning I had thirteen missed calls before 7 a.m. from an unknown number. When I received another, I picked up the phone.

"I don't think you get it, Clarice! You have been asking for my devotion since the first week we were together. And I have realized I want to marry you, for fuck's sake! I made *one* mistake."

"I'm not going to marry you. I'm going to block this number," I said. "Stop getting burners."

"Come down and talk to me, just listen to me."

"What do you mean, 'come down'?" Maxine leaned against my doorway with a bowl of overnight oats and mouthed, "You okay?" I shrugged. She shrugged. I waved her away.

"I've been walking around your block since four in the morning," P.T. hissed after a pause. I got a sudden sense of dizziness when he said it. I sat down in silence at my desk chair. Tried to consider how this could be seen as normal to him, as romantic, as persistent, as a fight for love.

"I'm devastated, Clarice." I heard the pain in his throat. "The connection we have is rare. I know this, I'm older than you."

"By three years! You didn't even want to be in a relationship most of the time."

"That was then!"

"If you are outside my place when I leave for work, there's going to be a problem."

I called into my office and said we had a leak in the ceiling at my apartment so I would be late. I waited for hours. Still, when I left, P.T. was down the block, outside my subway station, his face flushed. I turned back toward my house, picking up speed, and he ran after me.

"Clarice!" he screamed, loud enough for me to stop and turn around. I didn't want to completely freak out the parents with their strollers, the elderly people walking, the delivery people delivering, all going about their ordinary business.

"You know that everyone thinks you are being too harsh?" he said, breathing too heavily from such mild exertion.

"Who is 'everyone'?" I said, incredulous.

"My therapist, my mother, my friends—" He looked down at his old, peeling loafers.

"What therapist? What *friends*?"

"They all think you're being insane," he went on. "They are suggesting I send you these gifts, try to contact you. I'm tormented."

"Okay, well, you ask this 'therapist,' if she had a client who asked her ex to stop talking to her, and he kept calling from different phone numbers, and texting, and sending letters, and multiple gifts, and gargantuan cookies, then reached out to her friends, then showed up at her house . . . you ask her what she would tell her to do."

"Don't say ex."

"Jesus Christ."

"Clarice, we need each other! Everyone's a loser except you and me!"

"No." I squeezed the bridge of my nose and briefly closed my eyes. "We're losers, too."

"Why can't you just listen to me?" he shrieked, and leaned against an unwell oak that stood next to the entrance of my building, marked for removal.

"I've heard what you've had to say, P.T. Multiple times."

"Why can't you just give me a chance?"

I took a breath, let it out. "Because I fucking hate myself when I'm around you."

I turned back into the apartment to the sound of an inhuman wail. It was the last thing I would ever say right to him, straight to his face. But even then, even as he was starting to really disturb me, disgust me, I felt a persistent sense of grief and something resembling tenderness. I didn't want him to lose control. I wanted someone to help him, some witch to place her hands on his head and release every dark thought or compulsion he had, to liberate them with abrupt force, like a flock of birds all leaving the same tree at once.

4

I don't tell Roz, my therapist in LA, that I saw P.T. I tell her that I *thought* for a brief second I saw P.T. but then immediately realized it was "a trick of the light and psyche" inside a shitty bar on the eve of Halloween. I usually don't edit myself with Roz at all, but today I do. It's been a week now and I've tried to compartmentalize and ignore. Somewhat successfully. And by that, I mean I've been taking weed gummies and removing Instagram from my phone every other day. Roz says that the faux sighting makes sense this time of year. She says it sounds like I had found myself, once again, as Bunny's third wheel, and that probably didn't feel great. *Did it cause you shame that you were on someone else's date?* she asked, too bluntly. Guilty as charged! She often tells me I should think of my refusal to engage in romantic intimacy not as a weakness—or a curse—but as proof of violation.

Today we're on a Zoom call, doing inner-child work together. This more or less means limping through foggy recollections of bad childhood memories and visualizing different outcomes. This will lead me, in the future, to make different, safer choices. Or something. As an accessory to the practice, she encourages me to do childish, playful things out of session. Color, buy toys, eat Froot Loops for dinner. Today we return to kindergarten. She takes me into a meditative state, asks me to sink into a bad memory we've chosen together, then I will create a lovelier scenario for my inner child. Roz and I save the five-year-old version of myself from a wooden chest I accidentally locked myself in, and fainted inside, while my parents were having a physical altercation. One catalyzed by a disagreement about who played the father in *Ordinary People*. (Donald Sutherland.)

I decide to bring "small me" out of the bedroom chest while still conscious. I give her a bubble bath. I take her to a fancy hotel swimming pool. We eat a layered caramel cake while lounging on pool floats shaped like happy gators. Then a shadowy figure arrives, which sometimes happens when I create these safe spaces. He takes a piss in the water. Roz slowly guides me out of the meditation after I mention the piss. When I open my eyes, she asks me why I think someone invaded my scene.

"Actually, I think I do know," I say, clearing my throat, preparing for a half-truth. "My dad texted me last week." I rearrange myself on my couch. It's true, he did, and it unsettled me, but I'm guessing P.T. is the actual reason for this imaginary intruder.

"You're only mentioning this now?" she asks, reaching beyond her screen to grab what appears to be a thick, mud-colored smoothie in a blender bottle. "What did the text say, Clarice?"

"It said, *we cool?*"

"'We cool?'" she repeats, seeming confused. According to Damian, my dad has exceptionally bad motor skills since his aneurysm—like can't-always-hold-on-to-cups bad—so the very act of texting is in and of itself surprising. We haven't spoken in three years. I didn't think he had a phone anymore, and his girlfriend, Winnie, a young and ambitious real estate agent, works a lot, leaving him alone with his nurse in their house in Yonkers.

"What do you think about his reaching out, Clarice?"

"He must use talk-to-text," I say. I want her to laugh. She doesn't. "I don't know what I think. I guess that I still feel ill when we have any kind of interaction. I figured he was calling to tell me he was dying, so I texted Damian."

Dad texted me. Dying?

You forgot his birthday

Uhhhhhhhhhhhhhhhh?

For what it's worth he probably doesn't have all that much time left.

shame

your anger is justified.

Although your tone still comes across as callous?

sure sure sure

V Scorpio move of him tho right

calling fully estranged kid to chastise for no bday card :(

He's selfish.

is that what they call brain damage now

Incapacitated or not, it was classic my dad, a man who'd last remembered my birthday a decade ago. He had wished me a "Happy 19th" for the third year in a row. Accompanied by a crisp twenty bucks and the same joke: *One for good luck*. It was so demented I had to think he intended to humiliate me.

"No, I guess we forgot his birthday," I tell Roz now. I rub a dart of pain in the back of my neck.

"And do you know how it was he sent the text? Do you think it was Winnie who sent it?"

"I'm sticking to the talk-to-text theory."

"Well, I sense there's a connection between your father's call and seeing the P.T. look-alike. Does that resonate?" she asks, once again with the smoothie. She shakes it back and forth, then gulps.

"Yeah, I've got stuff lurking in there, Roz," I say, laying my head back against my pillow and letting out a belly breath.

"I know you cringe when I say this, but these are the moments when you turn to the spiritual," she says. "You were not protected as a kid, that's why they lurk. A higher power is a space to cultivate safety, Clarice."

"I think history has proven there's not anything keeping anyone safe, Roz," I say, and as always, she tells me that's the core belief we have to tackle.

After my therapy session, I see Bunny has texted me an article about how, from an evolutionary standpoint, people have never worked from the same place they sleep until recently. She's been on one with me and my well-being since I had the "migraine" at Afterlife. I'd rather want to kill myself for a few days each month than "curate a home office" or rent a coworking space like she wants me to do.

I read about this novelist I love who worked from bed, Bun. It's all good.

was that novelist Sylvia Plath?

no and enough with Plath suicide jokes! People gotta let her rest.

That said, I get up and decide to work from the little courtyard at the Los Feliz public library. Today I will heed her advice because she might be right. Perhaps staying inside for so long, is, in fact, worsening my anxiety. Bed-working and night-living were things P.T. and I had in common. When we started dating we'd talk on the phone until dawn. We'd watch movies all night, make playlists. Even if we weren't drinking we would wake up around dusk feeling hungover.

I try to shake off the thought of him. My neighbors—the Screaming Birds—are having one of their fights while the pet parrot squawks. Going past their door, I am faced with the rotting earth–and–syrup smell of bird shit and a fifty-fifty chance I'll bear witness to a murder-suicide. Funnily enough, I didn't notice how clearly you can hear them from my apartment when I have the windows open until Bunny pointed it out once when she was over.

"You're actually able to ignore that?" she asked me.

"The chemical smell?" I responded. "It's a new tile cleaner."

"The . . . sound of that man threatening to kill his girlfriend in her sleep?"

I stopped for a moment, listening.

"Oh. Oh, yeah. I guess I can hear it."

"Does that happen a lot?"

"Yeah, now that I think about it? It didn't register."

Bunny gave me a soft smile. She knew it was noise I was used to, perhaps that soothed me in some perverse way. It was what I heard in the womb. Then part of the way I learned how to talk. And then, more or less, how I learned to be in love. P.T. and I had screamed at each other all the damn time.

Ever since she pointed it out, I hear them whether I want to or not, particularly all the insane things he says to her about how ugly she is and how he wishes she would drop dead. You'd think Screaming Bird Guy would be nine hundred pounds of pure muscle, built like a '70s Cadillac, gold teeth, but he's delicately boned, short, candle yellow, and of indeterminate age. I've only seen Screaming Bird Guy's face once; usually he's got a cap obscuring his face like he's some minor celeb. She's fleshy with long brown hair, always wearing skirts to the ankle. Screaming Bird Girl's voice is, devastatingly, unfortunately, gentle. Brings to mind Melanie Griffith. She says hello sometimes at the mailbox, without looking at me, and it floats from her mouth as though her voice, too, is a fledgling.

As I'm locking my door I hear him tell her he doesn't care if he goes to jail. The Screaming Bird Girl murmurs inaudibly. Then something hard hits a wall. Luckily it sounds inanimate, but still, it stops me in place. I'm wearing clogs—a faux pas my cantankerous downstairs neighbor never fails to point out by pounding a bat on his ceiling each time I wear them. But it means I will be announcing myself to the Screaming Birds as I walk past, an unwelcome reminder they are being witnessed. If there's one thing I learned from my dad, it's to never embarrass a shitty man when he's pissed.

I think about going back in to change my shoes, but then Screaming Bird Guy kick-slams open his door as I hear her call out, "Come back!" He stomps out of the building, looking, if I'm honest, like he's on his way to get a crowbar.

I can hear her mewling as I pass. I take a deep breath and consider my options. I'm afraid to get involved but also don't want blood on my hands, or to feel this sense of sorrow for her, or to call the cops. On a previous occasion, when things sounded particularly bad, I googled "what to do if your neighbor is being abused" but there were just a few hotline numbers and a couple Reddit threads arguing about the efficacy of the police. I decided to go ahead and call a hotline.

"Hey, um, what do you do if you hear people fighting?" I asked when I got through.

"What kind of fighting are you hearing?" said a kind volunteer with vocal fry.

"Like bad. Threats, thuds. Wild animal sounds made by humans."

"Are you calling for yourself, hon?" I heard her quietly snap some gum in the back of her mouth.

"No, it's these people in my building."

"Honestly, I know it sucks," she told me, "but this is for people in search of their own help."

Perhaps today I can heave-ho the responsibility onto Courtney, our well-intentioned but inept building manager. Bless her soul, but she still hasn't gotten someone to properly fix the handle on my toilet, which has now flooded multiple times (this also incurred some noisy umbrage from below), so she owes me one. I ascend to Courtney's apartment on the fifth floor and consider how there seem to be many solo dwellers in my building. I wonder if that's an omen for me. If there's some spiritual significance. A girl down the hall has performatively loud sex, and there's the Screaming Birds, and one burnout couple with a baby, face tattoos, and a commitment to EDM that tempts me to kidnap and raise their child on my own—but as for everyone else, I don't know. Lots of solitude. But despite that, and despite living next to a Shakey's Pizza Parlor, and despite having my car broken into twice in a year, I feel comfortable here. It feels, or felt, like it would be impossible for anyone to find me.

When I get to Courtney's door and knock, she's not there. Which means it is, once again, on me. I go back down, and it's completely silent now. Actually more concerning than the cries and whimpers. I knock on the door. And then I knock on the door again, a little faster.

"Hello," she says eventually, in her tiny way.

"Hey, this is Clarice from one oh eight," I say, and add, "The girl with the loud shoes?"

A heavy pause. I hear bird wings flapping, I hear her sniffles. "I know who you are."

"This is maybe weird, but I wanted to say hi."

She's silent and I hear her sniffling again. "Okay."

"Okay, cool." I twirl my key chain around my pointer finger, nervous. "I thought I would mention that I live here. If you want, like, help or anything."

I'm met with more silence. Of course now I feel like a fucking imbecile, some meddling weirdo who should understand that violence is a part of life and also none of my business.

I step away just before the front door to the building opens again, forcefully, and the Screaming Bird Guy is back. He is angry still, but a little less so. He looks past me down the hall like there is no other human in sight. I go slack and still as he passes me. I take a deep breath and notice my hands are shaking.

5

It was Maxine who finally convinced me to report P.T. to the police. To put things on the record. She was no fan of the cops but said doing that was a necessary step if things escalated and I needed to go to court—her cousin with the poisoned dog learned that the hard way. She told me that this was the point where I could make a choice. Look at the facts and react before something went terribly wrong. I said if I was overreacting, it could really fuck him over. I was starting to call out sick from work because I was depressed. I lied, telling them I had an autoimmune disorder, that something was wrong with my blood. Maxine would text me during the day from her work computer in the living room while I stayed in bed, streaming old sitcoms.

What if you underreact, ever thought of that?

It's not like he's threatening to hurt me or kill me

Watch a few true crime shows about domestic murders.

See how it starts. You think he'd leave a paper trail with threats?

He's sharp

Right but. I don't know if I'm in
danger, so I don't want to do anything
excessive

Excessive. Right.

I don't know!

It's danger ok

He's infiltrating your work, your friends, your
family, your house.

Just sending all this shit at you.

the same fucking thing

over and over and over

It's lunacy

It is un damn hinged

and the fact that you "don't know" if you're
in danger is what makes it emotional
terrorism

You think I'm emo terrorized?

You're having nightmares, you're depressed,
you won't date, you're raggedy

bizarre eating habits

this is all textbook

um rude

I know you're right. I just want him to stop without having to do something drastic

And how will you make that happen?

You gave every opportunity for that

Yeah, maybe a little more time?

Don't let it play too far

men who can't listen

It don't end well

I am TELLING YOU

Please don't try to scare me

I'm TRYING to get you to respect yourself enough to keep yourself safe

options are limited with this shit . . .

plus cops actually help white girls sometimes, you know that?

damn

Then Maxine told me if I really didn't believe he was being all that creepy, that I should make a list of what he's done, look at it, and ask myself what might happen next that would make me uncomfortable enough to take action. So I did that. And while I looked at the list, I thought, damn, it really does take a lot of convincing. And even after you're convinced, and the people around you are convinced, and perhaps the evidence is there, it's still hard to believe it's necessary to do something. This is just how people behave sometimes.

The next day, Maxine and I decided to go to the precinct closest to our house.

"You're going to let him win?" Maxine said when I came out of my room, looking me up and down. I was holding a melted Dunkin' iced latte from yesterday and was still wearing the sweatpants I'd slept in. She was right, I had stopped putting any effort into my appearance. Luckily it was winter so I could cover up in a puffer and some large, dark scarves, but even those items were getting donut-glaze stains. I stopped highlighting my hair, letting it go unbrushed before shoving my mousiness into a haphazard ponytail. Two large college hoodies were getting a lot of play.

"Looks aren't everything," I told her.

"But they're something," she said.

No matter the hour, Maxine was always in an outfit with matching shoes, her hair in a tight bun at the nape of her neck. She wore a lot of thoughtfully collected Dries Van Noten. She was a self-taught entrepreneur, so her success was something she took rightful pride in. She couldn't comprehend how I had the gall to look so pitiful, especially since I had the means to dry-clean a good sweater. Usually Maxine didn't suffer fools or whiners or white girls—of which I was all three—but we'd both had shitty childhoods, so she gave me a bit of leeway. We would make hideous jokes with each other about having abusive step-parents, addict fathers (her dad had been an evil-seeming pill-popper doctor)—stuff you absolutely can't say around people who grew up happily. I don't know if she truly liked me or just felt sorry for me, but I do know she was invested in my survival. And when she said something wasn't my fault, ultimately, I believed her.

I went up to the front desk, behind a bulletproof partition like they have in liquor stores. The front desk cop didn't look at me when she told me she'd be with me in a minute. The moment I sat down, she told me she was ready.

"*This* bitch," Maxine said under her breath as I walked up again.

After I told her I wanted to report someone who was harassing me "and like, kind of being stalky," she handed me a clipboard with prompts like "What happened?" and "Make a timeline." She pointed me into a tiny room and told me to fill it out and wait on a small wooden bench that was too low to the ground. Probably to make visitors feel diminutive. I tried to move to the metal folding chair in the corner, but she told me from the other room that it was for staff. I moved back to my bench and tried to describe, in the blank inches provided below each question, what exactly was happening. It felt stupid. I wrote "He seems off," then crossed it out. After a few minutes a woman sat down next to me and began writing furiously on a piece of paper, sniffing up snot from her nose. I was fascinated by the way she looked. Like the prototype for the Man's creation of woman: dollish, milk pale, lost, supple, cervine. She wore a wig, these massive eyelashes, robin's-egg-blue eye shadow. Rings on each long-nailed finger and a velour sweatsuit entirely in baby yellow. A showgirl from another world. She couldn't fully lift her gaze; in fact, her eyes seemed to face inward like she was watching her own thoughts. She whispered hello to me. I felt the uncomfortable urge to touch her—she gave off the scent of juniper and oranges. I tried to see what she was writing on her form with such vigorous concentration.

A different cop, Officer Ed, took my paper and told me to follow him into a dirty, nondescript office. He looked too young to have such damaged capillaries. When I suggested, out of nerves, that the other woman could go before me, he whispered that she came in every other day to report a guy she was married to and still lived with, still loved, whom she had an active restraining order against. He said some people can't help themselves. He'd get to it later.

"But, yeah, your guy here seems like a freak," he said as he sucked some air through his teeth and read, slowly, through the papers I'd filled out.

"Thank you, he is a freak," I said. He flipped it over and continued to read where I had taken a little more room to explain myself on the back.

"So, what does this say after the 'he sent me an ancestor massage'?"

"Ancestral release massage. He also sent tickets to Butoh—a dance concert."

"Do you know if this chump has access to firearms?" He waved his pen around like it was a casual question. Behind him there was a row of portraits of cops who'd lost their lives on the job. Kind of a lot of them.

"You think he's going to shoot me?"

"Of course he has access to guns." Maxine came in from the other room, having procured a bottle of Diet Pepsi. She belched a little inside her mouth, then slowly released it out the side.

"Yeah, I guess who doesn't," said Officer Ed, scratching hard at a spot above his pecs. "Anyway, before you hear another peep from this guy, I think you should go down to the court ASAP and get an order."

"A restraining order?" I said, craning my head at him.

"That's the one."

"What'd I tell you," Maxine said, leaving the room, shaking her head, taking a sip of soda.

I followed Maxine out of the station, passing the woman who was still in that little room. A man was now in there with her, and they were screaming at each other. She said something about his meth scars, he said something about her drinking directly out of the orange soda container.

We got out on the street and waited for the bus. Maxine's hands were in her cowhide coat, her hair so shiny it reflected the streetlight. Her breath hit the dark winter evening and rose.

"You've got stuff going on, I'm not saying you don't," she said, then nodded her head back toward the station. "But that woman we just passed? That's someone who is so fucked up in her relationship she can't function. That's someone who did not get out in time. That's not you. You understand that?"

"Well, we don't know her," I said, looking down to the ground and, like a kid, kicking some little rocks on the cement. "That's a lot of assumptions, Maxine."

I did get it, though. Whatever that woman got or would get, she did not get out in time. I felt like someone had sucked out my soul and replaced it with packing peanuts. I started to cry a little. "I know you're right." Maxine gave me a hard hug then, and an awkward pat on the shoulder.

"You know what I like about you?" she said. I shook my head and let the tears roll. "You're a mess, sure. But you're kind."

6

Are you totally certain?" Bunny slides a pair of jumbo purple Gucci frames atop her head to look me in the eye. She's chewing gum; I see flashes of hot pink in her mouth. "You got a good look at his face?"

It's oddly hot for November. We are sitting on striped towels at a private-seeming beach we like in Malibu, applying thick zinc to our arms and legs. The sun is a simple white dime in a cloud-free sky.

"Are you kidding?" I respond with a squeak. Bunny is scooping out sunscreen from underneath her periwinkle acrylics. "That's your *first* question?"

My chest gets tight at the doubt in her voice. It's now been sixteen days since the possible P.T. sighting. I really, truly held out for a while and stopped my online research, knowing it would yield me nothing but fear and obsession, but I started again this morning. I had a dream about him, woke up at 4 a.m. breathing rapidly, and now I can't stop thinking about him. Wondering if he knows where I am, if he might be staked out waiting for me somewhere nearby. It sounds ridiculous, and yet, I cannot for the life of me figure out what else he would be doing here. He literally hates the sun, it gives him a rash. He wouldn't be trying to make it in Hollywood. There's just no reason for him to be in Los Angeles. This morning, I got another odd "gift" at my door, an empty shoebox with pencil holes stabbed in the top. I have been obsessively searching the same nonsense over and over again on my phone ever since.

When Bunny pulled up to my place earlier I was sitting on my stoop looking at Instagram again, going over the same tagged photos I looked at on day one. I know I'll find something different, something will click. I want to keep the details of his life, the little I can find, fresh in my mind. I went back far enough that I was looking at things like a blurry group photo someone called @JimJimmer posted from a techno dance party P.T. attended in 2016. Before I met him. Then there was a picture @Hedon_Diane tagged of P.T. in late January—he's leaning on a wall outside a gas station. Two hot dogs for the price of one were being offered. I was afraid, because that could have been anywhere, but then I noticed it was a #TBT from #Hampshire. I put my phone away.

"A mistake, you know, is the best-case scenario," Bunny says.

"The best-case scenario is me hallucinating?"

"It's just surprising!"

"Yeah, it was really fucking surprising, Bun, that's why I disappeared from that ludicrous club." I lie back on my towel and pick up the book I brought. Bunny opens our cooler and snaps open a Coke. Skips songs on her playlist. I can tell she's itching to speak but doesn't want to be the first to crack. She does, finally.

"Maybe I don't want to believe it was him. And I feel like you were just talking about him a few days before you . . . saw him. No?"

"I noted that pause," I say, even more annoyed than I anticipated. "But hey, maybe it was a fucking doppelganger."

"Well, you do have that thing where you misidentify people sometimes—"

I cut her off. "I know what he looks like." I was not expecting to have to defend myself. I was expecting to have to calm her down. "And I know how he moves, Bunny. And how he flirts, which he was doing with the bartender."

"Sorry," Bunny says, taking another deep breath. "I was just remembering, for example, the summer you kept seeing Channing Tatum in Quiznos, but then you asked him for a picture and it turned out he was a youth pastor?"

"Wow. Really won't let that one go." I shake my head and a bit of angry spit dribbles from my mouth. The indignity.

"It wouldn't be crazy to mistake him for someone and then spin out, okay?" Bunny looks over at me and I stare straight ahead. "You've got PTSD."

"Thanks for the diagnosis."

"You told me that!"

"Mmm." I did, but still.

"Do you think there's someone we could ask where he might be living?"

"Not that I can think of, Bunny. We never had mutual friends. He didn't really have friends," I say. "And I'm terrified of his mother."

"You could pretend to be someone else and call her," she says. I didn't think of that. Do I still have her number?

"I'm not going to do that," I say, scrolling through my contacts to see if P.T.'s mom—an icy, beautiful woman named Natasha—is still in there. She is not.

"It just would be insane, seeing P.T. in LA," she says with a little laugh. "He doesn't seem like someone who would do well in the sun."

"I have no idea where he lives," I snap back. "I haven't heard anything about him since we were in court two years ago."

"Have you looked online at all?"

"Yes, obviously. He's published poems. He hasn't posted much on Twitter or whatever the hell it's called in about a year. He was always a psycho about having pictures of himself online—he worried about fucking deepfakes. But I did find a picture of him tagged in California on Instagram."

"From when? And where?"

"Six months ago. Griffith Park, Bunny."

"I think you should cool it on the online research."

"Let's just drop it for now. You're making me feel stupid."

I turn my body away from her, start pretending to read again.

"I'm going to say one last thing," Bunny says. "I do not think you're crazy. But it's also possible, for the sake of optimism, that you made a mistake. And even if he's here? It doesn't mean he's here for you."

"Yup," I say, turning the music up on the little Bluetooth speaker. I look out at the rhythmic pull of the waves.

"Okay, actually, can I say one more thing?" Bunny says after we sit there for a good five minutes.

"What?" I'm feeling deep regret for mentioning this. It's likely she's right, because she is often right when I'm spinning out about something.

"Do you think maybe a little bit you might have wanted to see him? And that in some way, bringing the drama back up, maybe this is connected to not being able to date?"

"Not *wanting* to date, correction. But no, I didn't want to fucking see him."

"He was the last person you were with, that's all," she continues, "and you haven't been with someone in so long. Even though he was a legitimate nightmare, maybe there's an element of—not reminiscing, but fear of moving on? Like, this is a major stretch, but like, some kind of emotional version of how rape victims sometimes masturbate to the memory of rape? Or maybe, more like, you're too scared to feel something new, but you want to?"

"Are you drunk?" My chest feels like it's splitting open. "I am going to pretend you didn't say any of that, because I know you have my best interests at heart and you're an out-of-the-box thinker."

"Don't get mad at me, Clarice, I'm just talking it out with you!"

"Well, then, if it's not P.T., I have some other psychopath leaving weird shit outside of my apartment."

"Leaving weird shit like what? What are you talking about?"

I don't respond. I get up fast and brush the sand off my hands, toss my sunglasses onto the towel, make a beeline toward the water. It's not that what Bunny said isn't plausible; it is. It's just supposed to be the last thing she suggests, not the first. She should have started with: "Let's find and destroy him." Usually she is so gentle in how she says things, so very much on my side. But every now and then, she slaps me. Not intending to be harsh. Just being honest. Still, even when I'm the one who's mad at her, I have this low-simmering fear she's going to tire of my bullshit and disappear. Even with Bunny, who has never wavered in our friendship since we met the first day of college, I worry about this. Bunny, who told me once junior year that she was in love with me. We were both wasted one night after we got back to our dorm room and she kissed me. I felt this odd sense of overwhelm at the idea of being with her, like drowning, like it was too precious an area for me to bring in the horrors of coupling. She was, and still is, the most unconditional form of love I've ever experienced. It's more true love than some people ever get. The fact that I wasn't drawn to her romantically, sexually, meant more to me. It was a connection that wasn't based in fear. Bunny is the one person who shows me repeatedly that love does not have to be foundationally sad. That love isn't always a process of grieving the space between you and someone else. Anyway, she shrugged off the rejection easily. She went for a semester abroad in Colombia, mainly to visit the city where she was adopted, and by the time she came back, it was like it never happened.

Recently she sent me a YouTube video from a life coach about how some people choose to be celibate as a way of getting to know themselves. In the end these people find a greater connection. She said, "Perhaps that's what you're doing. But, like, not intentionally." I considered the idea, but the person in the video, a former Unilever executive with new cheekbones and six kids who had relocated to French Polynesia, framed celibacy like it would be a challenge. It was not a challenge for me.

Sometimes, losing my desire feels more liberating than concerning. After a few months of dealing with P.T.'s harassment, I realized my libido had disappeared. I didn't want to be touched, let alone date. I could and can think of nothing less appealing than the process of "getting to know" someone. I remember in my mind what it's like to want, but my body can't muster up the sensation. In the place of wanting there's something like static, or a sense of being scraped out with the serrated precision of a grapefruit spoon. It's not clear what is left of me.

Bunny frequently reminds me that love is as necessary as air. *Love is the thing*, she always says, sounding like the disembodied narrator on a dating reality show. And I'm like, *What kind of love constitutes "the thing"?* I love her, I love Damian, I love watching TV. That's my thing. Monks and nuns love God. That's their thing.

But again, as eager to explore, as "open-minded" as Bunny is, she's never truly understood what happens to me when that valve is really turned on. What I want when I want is not good, I've told her. My want means attaching myself to a person who fundamentally can't give me care, then I debase myself while I try to force it out of them. I have the potential to spend my whole life wanting, trying, and failing to get through to someone. That instinct does not need to be freed up. Not wanting to do that is my achievement. It's easier than having to constantly fight against my nature.

So this suggestion that my "spotting" P.T. is further proof that I'm love-starved feels like a real fuck-you. I'm not so delusional that I want P.T. to move to LA, skulk around, and leave puzzling objects outside my apartment door in an effort to win my affections. If he is back, he's back because the reality is that sometimes bad things don't go away.

I come to from my thoughts when I get the sense someone's looking at me. My feet are burning cold, I'm standing ankle-deep in frigid water. Next to me stands a guy staring so intently at me that I'm both embarrassed and assume he has mistaken me for someone else. He's got a Medusa tattoo on his biceps and hair on his chest, and he's in printed surf trunks. I have an impulse to shove him or scream at him to fuck off. My period is near so my boobs are huge, all but fighting their way out of the top of my suit, which is the only reason I can imagine he might enjoy the sight of me in a swim-team-grade black Speedo. I give off a sexual vibration akin to touching twin poles in two magnets, a tangibly resistant but invisible force. Bunny tells me people check me out more than I think they do, I just don't notice inside my mental fortress. But this guy's presence hovers invasively, like a bad smell. I can tell he wants something from me, it's that kind of anticipatory silence. I'm uncomfortable, getting nervous, honestly, and I'm finding it hard to move. When I glare at him, trying to emanate a willingness to fight him if necessary, he smiles and points out to the horizon. He's showing me a pod of dolphins who are cruising along, taking turns propelling themselves out of the water.

"My wife told me dolphins communicate telepathically, did you know that?" he says as we stand there, unmoving, watching their little fins pop in and out. I was preparing to bolt like I was being hunted. In reality this random man is trying to share the wonder of nature with the person who happens to be next to him.

“I think I’ve heard that before,” I manage, barely audible. I think of something Roz reminds me of frequently, a disappointing, cliché bit of truth. *You have a deep-seated fear of men. It becomes resentment.* I tell her how pathetic that sounds, an aversion to men, how it paints me as the proverbial old maid. I wish I were afraid of something less embarrassing, like ghosts or death.

I say nothing else to the man in shorts, just walk into the waves and dunk under, not able to suppress a yelp of pain when I reemerge. Despite the cold, there’s nothing better than the second you rise from the sea. It puts things in perspective. I consider the ocean forgiving of human folly in that it doesn’t register a person, it has no regard for selfhood, it’s kindly on offer while also plainly able to destroy you. I close my eyes like it will help me disappear. I’d like to be transported into the crevasse of a canyon or a sea-adjacent cave, curled up on a flat rock covered in algae, waves lapping at me, the sound of my breathing the only thing I can or will ever hear again.

Do you know that guy?” Bunny asks with a flirtatious upward tilt to her voice as I burrow my face into a towel to dry off.

“Who? The guy in the shorts?”

“Yeah, I thought I saw you talking,” she says.

“Oh, no, there were dolphins out there,” I say. “He pointed them out.”

“He’s cute.”

I put my sunglasses on and place my hat on top of my face. “I guess if you like that kind of thing.”

“Who doesn’t?”

I say nothing, bite into an apple, take out my book.

It’s quiet between me and Bunny the rest of the day. I can feel her anxiety hovering. The air feels particularly thick with salt.

I don't know what to say, Clarice," she says, idling outside my door, despite a Dodge Charger revving behind her, laying on the horn. She shoots her arm out the window, gives a fierce, annoyed wave. Her earrings are swinging when she turns back to me.

"Neither do I," I say, looking away from her.

"I don't think you're nuts, obviously." Bunny turns the volume of the music down. "I also don't think you need to be scared."

I stay silent and she adds, "I think it's a really good idea to just pretend it didn't happen and let it go." We look at each other for a beat and I give her a nod, then a halfhearted kiss on the cheek.

The sun is about to set, which is a weird time in East Hollywood—it feels like the whole neighborhood exhales, ready to relax. Every evening a bunch of people roll into the Shakey's parking lot next to my building and sit there for hours, order fried chicken with huge sodas, blast bass, smoke pot, and scream-laugh. Clusters of elderly people perch in lawn chairs on the sidewalks or on their balconies, just watching. A thousand people arrive home from work, all walking their dogs at once. Instead of going inside, I sit on the stairs outside. I consider that Bunny is probably right about one thing, that the best thing to do would be to pretend, at least for now, that this isn't happening. I take out my phone and see a slew of texts and a missed call from Damian.

So. Mom's wedding.

What are you thinking about it?

Are you triggered?

Clarice?

I would appreciate responses to my calls and texts.

Was at the sea, sorry bro

What about it?

Are you attending?

. . . of course

This is not to be read in critical tone, C.

Don't always know your willingness level when it comes to parental involvement

I like mom! most of the time.

And not triggered

mitch is our best dad yet

Yes, Mitch seems to be a stand-up gentleman.

Just confirming . . . as it would be a challenge to confront the experience alone.

I would have driven to LA and forcefully placed you into my vehicle.

Honestly I'd love a ride

Fair warning, she did mention something to
me about asking you to sing.

fully demented

not a chance in hell

I'm tone deaf.

I remembered this and informed her.

I consider talking to Damian about seeing P.T. The likelihood is that he would be levelheaded about it but still concerned, and I think he would believe me. We went through enough as kids to know that it's astonishing how sinister the universe can get. But it would just be another thing to add to his proverbial ulcer. He doesn't express extreme emotions like panic, grief, or exaltation, instead has IBS and chronic TMJ, and wears a government-issued uniform in his chosen profession.

I hear a throat clearing and look up from my phone. The Screaming Bird Guy has come out here at some point. He's facing away from me, out to the street. Wearing a pair of Adidas slides, no shirt. I can smell the thick fresh soap and skunk smell of good weed.

"Can you believe it's November and it's this hot?" I say, immediately nervous. He shrugs. We both watch two old Armenian men across the street, also smoking. One of them is laughing so hard he starts to cough, the other one smiling smugly.

"You know my girlfriend, right?" The Screaming Bird Guy doesn't turn to face me when he asks.

"Um, not really, no," I say slowly. "I mean, I've seen her around."

"Oh, she said you two know each other." He takes another

long drag and makes a loud rasp when he exhales, hard, like something got caught. He cracks his knuckles, and I sense it's something he does to abate his temper.

"Oh well, yeah, I mean, we've talked," I say. I'm worried now that anything I say will be used against her. If I say yes, we're conspiring. If I say no, she's a liar. "And maybe it was her—yes, it must have been—who I borrowed some milk from a while ago." He's quiet and I feel my heart start to beat harder.

"We don't drink milk," he tells me, after a long pause. "We never buy it."

"Yeah, well," I say, suddenly annoyed. "Neither do I."

I brush past him with no destination in mind. Of course the Screaming Bird Guy chooses now to try to subtly intimidate me—because I'm sitting here, bone-tired and weary, so much so that the trip from Bunny's car into my apartment felt like it required a break, and that weariness, in one way or another, is because of men like Screaming Bird Guy, who drill their way into your brain until you're crazy and cause you a kind of fear so deep it never leaves, only sleeps. I was just trying to get a breather from Bunny's disbelief, from going inside and doing more directionless P.T. research. If I really drag it out, that exhaustion is bundled up with shitty boyfriends, and the one good boyfriend whom I left for no reason, and multiple booze-fueled "were they assaults?" at parties, and the pictures of spread-legged women with curtain bangs my grandpa showed me when I was a kid, the legitimate collection of offenses from various stepfathers, the interminable problem of my dad in both presence and absence, and damn, even Dad's dad, Grampy Chip, who came back from World War II with PTSD, a head wound, and a drinking problem. Probably Grampy's dad, too, Pappy Howard, who shot himself through the mouth and left Grampy with a mother who smacked him all the time. I carry my mom's damage, and her mother's, too. That's why people talk about epigenetics all the time, isn't it? The reason you are the unfortunate way you are, it's got to be transgenerational stress inheritance. An ancestor's past trauma changes the way your body reads your DNA—parts of the sequence get marked chemically like an asterisk on part of a recipe, and the notation on the DNA, so to speak, the revised instruction, can get passed to your progeny, just like cancer. The damage is reversible, so says Roz, in a sort of "the buck stops here" plug for therapy. And that's been my mortal assignment this go-round, I guess, since my dad was a bust and my mom certainly didn't heal too much, or didn't know how, so it seems I arrived on Earth with the photographer who repeatedly groped her during a modeling shoot for Maybelline already in my wiring (maybe she's born with it?); the strange lurker who attacked her and ripped open her shirt while pushing her against the exterior of a closed laundromat (she escaped when she shoved her key into his groin and stomped on his arch with her heeled boot, then sprinted with the capable legs she had acquired playing tennis); the theater director, age eighty, who fingered her in a nightclub under the table so hard he made her bleed. *I think I agreed to that*, she told me once. *But I'm not sure.* This kind of thing, written in the blueprint. My father's past, too, written in, whatever the fuck was done to him, what he did to others, then would do to me. This collection of emotional detritus is probably what brought me to P.T. in the first place, and if I'm not careful, this is what will keep him with me forever.

When I eventually get back home, just as the sky is lowering into night, walking down the hall of my apartment building through the thick scent of red sauce, I see something from a distance. I get to my door, and sitting outside my apartment, there's a pair of binoculars. No note. No box. Just sitting on the floor. I pick them up, notice they're antiques, they're creepy, and they're not mine. I get this dreadful sting in my belly, because this one truly reeks of P.T. A gift and a threat—his modus operandi.

Strangely, even more than fear, what comes to mind when I look at the binoculars is a good time we had. One that, in retrospect, seems foreboding. We were in Prospect Park in spring, walking one of the short trails that weave through and bring you to unexpected little enclaves. We came to a grassy clearing between the trees. P.T. said it was the perfect time of year to find four-leaf clovers. He crawled on his hands and knees while I lay back on the grass with my eyes closed, feeling peaceful. "Lookie here," he said, and I squinted up at him. He was holding three four-leaf clovers. I said I thought those were nearly impossible to find. "You can find anything if you really look for it," he told me. He handed me one and put the other two in his mouth, chewed, and swallowed.

7

Maxine and I both took off work the day I decided to file a restraining order. I didn't know how to thank her so I bought her breakfast at a fancy French café a few blocks from the courthouse. "An incongruous pre-court hang," she said, cutting into a Croque Madame. "But this béchamel is fire."

I had still been receiving emails from strange addresses that I didn't open but didn't erase—Maxine said to keep all evidence. We went through a metal detector. A woman in front of me emptied her pockets and quietly asked what I was in here for. I told her I was considering filing a restraining order against someone. She moved through the detector and told me she had spent the last six months trying to obtain a restraining order against her alcoholic, abusive ex-wife.

"You just go in today and state your case," she said. "Tell the judge what he's been doing. It will be the first of ten thousand fucking times you'll have to describe it. You think you're sick of the story now? Give it a few months."

My skin felt itchy as she spoke. Maxine was scrolling on her phone and sending work emails. She was helping a client choose logo designs for a line of digestive supplements, and now and then would hold up the phone to ask my opinion. I wanted to be anywhere else. It occurred to me that there are few circumstances in life where one so viscerally feels what they can and can't control. Being in a courthouse, trying to attain a restraining order—you really feel the limitations of the physical world.

Maxine and I went up to the third floor. Family court. It was extremely sleek up there, white marble floors and what looked like marble walls, too. I imagined my teeth shattering. It was bright but windowless, clean shining overhead lighting. Outside the numbered wooden doors to the courtrooms were pews. The waiting room to heaven, and yet. The air was sucked out of the place. Inhumanely immaculate. State emblems on the wall. We passed young pro-bono lawyers in work casuals preparing their scared and/or fatally bored clients.

We sat in front of door six. A security guard came from the room to call the next person. I shot up in anticipation, but it wasn't me. It was some guy. I went into the steel and blue bathrooms and found vomit floating still as a lake in the toilet.

"Someone puked in there," I said to Maxine, who had switched from working to chatting on Hinge.

"Thanks for letting me know," she said.

Who knows how much time passed, but I finally went in. Maxine took a seat behind me, chest puffed, phone gone, a stoic expression. The judge's name, I saw, was Judy. What a cross to bear.

Judge Judy's questions were blunt and fast. A real guilty-until-proven-innocent vibe. I tripped up a little when she started rapidly questioning me. What are you here for. Explain the timeline. What did he do. How did he try to contact you. Has he threatened you. In what way did you tell him to stop.

"Well, I told him to stop, multiple times, verbally, and in written form. Forms, really. And so did my brother. And my friend."

She paused. "You know this is not to be done out of spite, right?"

"Yeah, that's not what I'm doing," I said sharply. The anger gave me some verbal motion. She remained silent as I spoke, her eyes slitted in what appeared to me an accusatory way. So I was surprised when she said she'd give me the temporary order of protection, and that it would be served to him, by the sheriff's office, over the weekend. I felt a momentary burst of relief until she told me that I would have to return in ten days in order to extend it. He would have to be there, too.

"In here? Together?"

"That's generally how these things go," said the Honorable Judy. "He will have the chance to respond to your claims."

I heard Maxine say, "That son of a bitch." The security guard who brought us in looked down at the ground to hide a smile.

"The date for our next hearing, to extend the order of protection, will be January thirty-first."

I let out a moan. "Can we do another day?" I rubbed my eyes with my palms, and added, weakly, "That's his birthday."

"January thirtieth," she said, once again surprising me. "You can pick up your papers on the second floor." The gavel sounded. Who knew they really did that.

8

I get to Afterlife earlier than most other patrons, right when it opens, around 8 p.m. It gets busy around eleven, according to Google. I figure it will give me plenty of time to set up shop, be casual, have some drinks, and start really chatting up the bartendress P.T. was flirting with before she gets overwhelmed by Gen Z, in search of spiked twig tea and Heineken 0.0. Bunny, Screaming Bird Guy, and the binoculars have piled on top of each other today to give me new resolve to handle this. I can't be in a gray area, I can't just sit around pretending this isn't bothering me, that he's not infiltrating my thoughts. This woman has had contact with him. It's very likely that she won't remember him, certainly won't know anything about him unless he's a regular. But she's all I've got.

At the moment, the only bartender on the clock is a mean-eyed beanpole of a girl with white-blue hair and patches on the back of her work polo. She's wearing earbuds while she prepares for her shift and dramatically takes them out when I sit down on a stool to order. I am, in fact, the only person in the bar. I blush. She's much younger than me, in fact doesn't look old enough to drink, so immediately my intention to pump her for information feels creepy. Instead of asking about her coworker, I order a gin on the rocks. It's disgusting and not something I would normally order, but I figure it will lend a noir pallor to the evening. I have the idea, while I'm waiting, to look up one of those phone number information retrieval sites to see if P.T.'s number is connected to a current address, then remember I deleted his contact. That said, it does explain how he might know where I live.

The opening musical act of the night, SVELtE94, brings out a laptop, a mic, and one of those looping voice pedals. He hangs up a sheet behind him that says "BE UNGOOGLE-ABLE." The irony. He's kind of good, a dainty soprano who makes what I would describe as, I guess, sound effect collages? I clap loudly at the end of his seven-minute opening piece, surprising myself by how drunk I already feel.

By SVELtE94's third piece, I'm feeling impatient, perhaps already hungover. It's just past nine. I decide to make do with the bartender who is here and ask a few questions. Gotta play it as it lays. So I sidle over and slide onto the seat closest to where she is leaning against the bar, looking at her phone.

"I was here the night before Halloween . . . ," I say, launching right in.

"Cool?" she says.

". . . and there was a bartender here with red hair."

"Did you lose a credit card or something?"

"No, I'm wondering about that bartender."

"Amanda?"

"Yes, that's right. Amanda!"

"What about her?"

"When does she work, exactly?"

"Uh . . ." Her brow knits, and I watch her look over my shoulder, distracted. She pours a small inch of bourbon in a mug. I keep my eyes up, mostly, and pretend I'm none the wiser. "She works some nights. And doesn't work other nights."

"Helpful."

"I'm not in the information business, pal."

"Could you be?" I say, fishing into my bag.

"Depends."

"So, you're amenable to a monetary exchange?"

"It can't hurt."

"Bold," I say, now reaching into my back pocket, where I find the ten I'm looking for. I put it on the table. "Very seventies. You're lucky I had to park in a cash-only lot earlier."

She slips it into her own back pocket, expressionless.

"So, tonight," I ask her. "Is she coming tonight?"

"No," she answers.

"Okay. Tomorrow?"

"No, she's off for the week."

"Oh, shit."

"She doesn't date women, if that's what you're after. Fuck knows I've tried."

"Right, okay, drats." I do a weak shucks-punch gesture.

"I got the message after she started going home with a different dude customer every night."

"Oh?" I say. "That's a thing she does frequently?"

"I mean, I don't want to talk shit, obviously," she says, pouring a little more bourbon into that mug below the bar. I notice that her lipstick has worn away from her lips, the color only a bold outline of the edges of her mouth.

"Obviously." I nod.

"But, yeah. Oh, fuckin' yeah," she says. "And I can spot which ones she'll choose from a mile away."

"She's got a type?" I ask, so casually.

"Something in their eyes, I'd say? An animal hunger? I mean, there's a sadness to it, you know, from her side. Some individuals get a waft of attention and give out a free rail-pass to fucktopia," she says, her expression exasperated. Clearly I've hit a sore talking point with this young woman about Amanda's sex life. She's been waiting to unload.

"Yeah, people are, you know, weak," I say, trying to get on

her good side, keep her rolling. "Can't imagine the cretins who must try to pick her up."

"Oh, yeah. Ohhhh, yeah. Some real bruisers. And I try, like, once? To give her a casual kiss? You'd think I had tried to take her captive. She fucking screamed." She reaches for a damp rag and starts to wipe down the bar, a surface sticky enough that I feel my elbow skin might peel off when I attempt to move it. I notice the bartender looks over at the stage just as SVELtE94's interpretation of Billy Joel's "Vienna" hits a difficult note. She snorts.

"I actually think he's got something," I say. "But you see this shit all the time, you probably know better than me."

"Probably, yes." She chuckles. She has tooth gems. I chuckle.

"So, your colleague Amanda," I say, emboldened. "Does she have a last name?"

"I'm probably not going to give you the last name of my coworker. Someone it seems like you want to bone?"

"No, no, we just got along, we talked about books." I scratch my head and look at myself in the mirror lining the back of the bar. I can instantly tell I'm lying. "Thought she might want to join my classics book club."

"Amanda does not strike me as a reader." She smirks. I feel mildly indignant on Amanda's behalf. A couple sits down next to me and asks for two bottles of IPA and a bag of toasted lentil chips. She looks at them, says nothing, then looks back at me.

"You're welcome to come back to this place of business when she might be working."

"Which is when exactly?"

We look at each other, unmoving. I take out and slide another dollar toward her. She doesn't move. I slide over a five that she takes. Unbelievable.

"She's back the Saturday after Thanksgiving."

I thank her with a nod, then turn back on the stool to watch the stage, where SVELtE94 has made way for a woman called

Delicate Stephanie, who, confusingly, recites *The SCUM Manifesto* while playing Bach on a guitar covered in MAGA stickers. I've got adrenaline like I shot it intravenously—I'm getting close. Then the bartender taps on my shoulder to let me know that if I'm not planning to order another drink, it would be great if I could make room at the bar.

9

Today for my session with Roz, we are in person, in her office in San Marino. Something we do once a month in her sparsely furnished seafoam-colored room. It's golden hour and Roz is glowing. Finally, I feel compelled to tell Roz the truth—that I did in fact, almost definitely, see P.T. at the bar on Halloween Eve. I'm just having a little trouble getting it out. I've spent the first ten minutes of the session talking about whether or not I will stay home alone for Thanksgiving and asking Roz if she thinks I should get a cat. Eventually, she asks me what is really going on.

"You know how I thought I saw P.T."—I massage my forehead and avoid looking at her—"flirting with a female bartender?"

"Yes," she says. "Did you think you saw him again?"

"Well, no, but . . . I actually am almost sure, and was even sure then, that it really was him I saw. The real P.T., that night. I've been doing a lot of like . . . research, as a result." I still avoid eye contact. I don't want to interpret her expression and relatively neutral tone of voice.

"Oh? What kind of research?" Roz clears her throat.

"Well, at first, you know, just like internet stuff. Rather hard-core on that. Social media deep dives."

"And? What did you find out?" Her skirt makes a swoosh sound as she crosses her legs. I look up but not at her, notice through the large window behind her armchair that two birds land on a branch at the exact same time. Like some weird, malefic signal. Of what, who knows.

"He's published poetry. He identifies on social media as 'the truest leftist.' I went way back on Google search results. He had another lawsuit before we met, someone accused him of stealing a rare baseball card from a house party. Which, let's be honest, he probably did."

"Can I ask why you didn't tell me at first?"

"I don't know exactly. Then Bunny thought I hallucinated his face onto someone when I told her the other day. That made me feel nuts and sort of . . . out of control."

"Hmm." Roz readjusts herself ever so slightly. "I understand that. In the research, was there anything about his whereabouts? Or anything more specific? Job? Relationship status?"

"Not really. There was one tagged picture of him in LA that I found from six months ago, he was here with his cousin who lives in Seattle. I don't know what that means. Most everything else he posts online is characteristically abstract, and infrequent. And the pictures never really show his face, it's always from behind or looking down or artistically blurred. He was always weird about having his image online."

"I can't imagine the research was much fun," she says thoughtfully, after a beat. "That's not normally something you do."

"Yeah, no, I haven't googled him or Insta-stalked him since we broke up."

"That's a long time."

I feel my gut buckle a little when she says that. It's been a long time, she's probably thinking, so why am I still thinking about him?

"Have you tried to reach out in any capacity?"

"Oh, god no," I say.

"Good. I'm glad to hear that."

"The only thing I have done, if we're talking *any* capacity—

last night I went and inquired about the bartender he was talking to that night. She wasn't there, but I found out when she works and—"

"You're planning to go back to see her, Clarice?" Roz cuts me off to ask this. I'm taken aback.

"I'm thinking that's probably a bad idea?" I say, finally meeting her eye. It feels too much to look at her for long, it makes every possible scenario too real, so I look at the pastoral artwork on the opposite wall.

"What are you feeling now?"

"Bad, I guess," I answer, sullen. "Like I said, Bunny thinks I'm imagining things, or like, I don't know. Essentially that I'm repressed, horny, and afraid."

"What do you think?"

"Well, I think I'm pretty fucking sure I saw him."

"Okay, then more specifically, what are you feeling about having seen him then? In spite of what Bunny thinks?"

"I don't know. That I was thinking about him, I mentioned him just before I saw him. And that it's the time of year that we broke up, so that dredges stuff up. She thinks it's because I'm so subconsciously desperate for love I'm trying to squeeze something out of the last time I sort of felt it."

"Right." Roz takes a deep breath in, lets it out. She sits for a moment and does this thing she does while she's thinking: her eyes move back and forth. I always try to guess what she's thinking; I'm usually not right. Right now I'm thinking she's wondering how we've been working together this long and I'm still unwell, that perhaps she herself is a failure.

"Do you also think I'm projecting his face onto some other dirtbag at a bar?"

She laughs. "No, it very well could have been him, and it's just as possible it wasn't. We don't have enough information."

"Yeah," I say, disappointed.

"And if you yourself don't seem sure . . . ," she adds.

"What do you mean 'don't seem'? I said pretty fucking sure." I'm angry now. "What other information do I need than that to consider whether or not I'm safe?"

"Well, I trust your judgment, of course."

"It doesn't really sound like it."

"No, Clarice. I'm interested as to why you were reticent to tell me you thought it was really him. And I also think that whether it was him or not, the effects of what he did are still very real and very intrusive. It makes me angry to think, whether or not P.T. was there, that he can continue causing such upset."

She doesn't trust me, I don't trust me. I nod and decide to fall into one of the long patches of silence Roz lets me sit in, even in person. I pinch the tiniest bit of skin on my left hand between two nails, a nervous habit when I feel particularly overwhelmed. I try to concentrate again on the tree where the two birds were, just past Roz's head, like it might stabilize me somehow. Then I notice, on Roz's desk, a pile of holiday cards she's in the middle of filling out, a pile already stacked and stamped. They have a picture of a smiling cartoon star and say "Happy All-idays!" This is who I'm trusting to guide my life. A person who earnestly chooses that greeting card.

I hate that I'm still talking about P.T. I hate how many times I've said his name to Roz. Yet I still show up with the underlying hope that in one of these sessions the right interpretation of the past will act as a panacea. It could be time to admit that whatever we're doing here is not working, because I'm sick of slow-burn healing. I'm tired of feeling like I can't rely on my interpretation of things. Roz says no one is right all the time, that trauma can skew certain parts of our intuition. Maybe my relationships are all just a big misunderstanding, lensed through my damage. I was so sure that there was delightful electricity between me and P.T. when we were together, enough to withstand some pretty bad times. So sure.

And obviously there was some good there. I have some nice

memories, too. We walked from Manhattan to Brooklyn in the snow, soaking our shoes through, and upon arriving home he gave me four pairs of socks, made me cocoa out of melted Toblerone. We took MDMA and went to museums. He read me *Gravity and Grace. Human existence is so fragile a thing and exposed to such dangers that I cannot love without trembling.* Our habit of hiding in public bathrooms so he could finger me, his hand over my mouth. The one time he told me he was falling in love with me while we were riding the subway—I couldn't make eye contact with him because I was so uncomfortably elated. I knew it could be good between us, I really knew it, and I knew I wanted to find a way for it to stay that way. When I was away from him, I wanted to get back to him. When I came to his door again, or he to mine, or I saw him arrive, always late, at a restaurant or movie theater, shaking off rain like a dog, bickering with the bouncer at a concert—the world felt okay. The nervousness drained out of me like oil, I got a hit of peace. What was that? He could have been manic, high, barely talking and in a wretched mood, but still. There he was and I could relax. Eventually that pattern resulted in a sense of entrapment. I wanted out but I didn't know how. It felt like I was in too deep.

My mom told me once that when she was pregnant with Damian, the eve of the day she gave birth, she picked my dad up from a party at 2 a.m. He was wasted. She said she looked at him in the car, comatose, drooling, and thought: *Who in god's name is that* man? She added that the day they married, about a year later, under the arch of city hall, unknowingly pregnant with me, she looked him in the eye, smiled, and had the acidic urge to puke.

I asked her once why she didn't heed her own warnings. *Things that don't make sense, don't make sense,* she said. *It's the type of good instinct you don't realize you've had until later.* I didn't get that then, but I get that now. You can feel there's something wrong; doesn't mean you believe it or know what to do with it. There's some gnarly centrifugal force, your lover the axis. Plus, for her, finding someone to marry was simply a thing people did, so she felt she had to stick to it. She could make a family, be normal, have a house, a husband. I found it funny that she thought my dad would be the one to do this with, an addict she met doing a Beckett play in a black box theater. Dad was fired during the first week of rehearsals because he punched the stage manager, but not before getting my mother's number. Then again, I thought I could make some semblance of a normal life with P.T., too.

"Did I lose you?" Roz asks this, I assume, because she can tell she's lost me.

"Well, I guess, I'll tell you another much more concrete reason I think it's him," I say, feeling too warm. "Some creepy things happened at my apartment. Someone has been leaving shit outside my door."

"Human excrement?" Her neck shoots forward. I can hear wind chimes from the yard.

"No, no, like, someone left a weird book, some socks once, and some used Q-tips in an envelope. Some binoculars."

"Oh, I don't like this."

"God, don't say that."

"Why? It's eerie."

"I've started spinning out about it already. I don't know. I just keep thinking of the symbolism. Connecting the Q-tips to our relationship and stuff."

"Explain how the Q-tips might symbolize something?"

"I would complain about how messy he was. You know, shit streaks on towels, beard hair in the sink. That kind of thing."

P.T. was one of those guys who went through bouts of anti-self-care one might associate with the proverbial truck driver. He was cerebral to the point where his environment was the afterthought of an afterthought. My mother used to joke when I was a kid that I should have been born into a family that had a butler, and it's horrifying, but I started saying the same thing to him. He'd grumble and tell me if I didn't like how he treated his own house, maybe I shouldn't come over.

"Did you tell your landlord about these items?"

"I told the building manager. The only other culprit I can think of other than P.T. is this intense couple from down my hall."

"And why would they have a motive for that?"

"It's a long story."

"Well, I think that was the right thing to do. And perhaps—this is a decision you can make on your own, but I would contact the police, and describe all the things you described to me."

"Are you serious?"

"I'm saying this to be extra, perhaps overly, cautious. And I'm so sorry that happened."

I put my head in my hands and stay there. "Clarice?" Roz comes over to the couch and sits down next to me. I hear her open one of the tiny bottles of water she has and I stick my hand out for it. I drink nearly all of it down. I want her to believe me, I don't want her to believe me. I want to be right, I want to be wrong.

"Now you think it was him?"

"I wish I knew, Clarice," she says, getting up, sitting back in her own chair.

10

I find Valentini's contact information on a Reddit thread. He has multiple rave reviews. I send him an email at four in the morning asking him to meet with me tomorrow even though it's Thanksgiving, and to his credit or strangeness, he writes back immediately.

If it's an emergency/there are lives at stake, I will move my regular 10 AM and give it to you. Best, Valentini

That's the thing, I don't know if there are lives at stake, but to err on the side of caution, let's say that yes, there are. Thanks, Clarice

I'll see you at 10.—Valentini

Can we make it 11? Not usually a morning person.—Clarice.

No.—Valentini

I don't sleep, which has been par for the course lately. I leave at 8 a.m. and sit in the driveway of his condo complex in Torrance. At 9:30, I see a woman leave his place, heaving sobs. At 9:40 he sends me an email that he can see I'm here, to come in.

I lift my fist to knock just as he opens the door. He's worryingly pale, five feet six inches tops, has a mild hunch and a quiet voice. He's wearing an unintentionally tight sweater with noticeable moth holes. He looks like a middle school math teacher, not a "clairvoyant/clairsentient/medium" with an "international and celebrity clientele" who "asks $400 an hour."

"Clarice, yes?" he says. I nod and stick out my hand and he takes it into both of his. They are warm, squishy, not quite moist. He leads me down a dark hallway, a space with no art on the walls, and past his kitchenette, where I notice the limited counter space is taken up by a complicated filtration system.

"A Brita wouldn't do?" I say, nodding my head toward it, then immediately regret showing my critical nature so soon. It's better if he likes me.

"Seems you haven't heard about microplastics in the blood." He points me to a proudly pleather, dark red couch that seems far too sexual an object for such a monastic, mostly empty space. The shades are down. It's carpeted. Where most people would have a flat-screen is one of those old-school posters of the cat hanging off a branch that says "Hang In There, Baby."

"If you're wondering why it's so dark," he says, closing curtains over the already drawn shades, "it's because I get ill when I'm exposed to overhead lighting. Especially while receiving."

"Receiving?" I ask.

"Visions, dear," he says, lighting a huge pillar candle he takes from beside where I sit on the couch. He places it in between me and a folding chair where he'll sit. He switches on a nightlight near his table. It's shaped like a mushroom.

"So how did you figure out you could do this?" I ask.

"Clairvoyance is a pedestrian gift, really, it's just one that few people know how to cultivate," he says, shaking out his hands and wrists as he stands talking. "Especially men."

"Were your parents hippies or something?" I ask, taking off my coat, uncomfortably shifting around on the couch, which lets out noises of a quiet, weeping whale.

"Oh, god, no. I'm a Miami-born Big Ten graduate and

recovering Catholic!" He laughs. It's a line he's clearly delivered before.

"So how did you know what to do? With the gift?" I ask.

"I had a psychic family member. She took note when I was a small child—I started correctly predicting deaths and divorces in our neighborhood."

"Very impressive," I say, unnerved. No Tibetan prayer flags, no massive phalluses of selenite, no psychedelic paintings of auric figures skyrocketing toward the light of Source. The absence of sage stink and just the one candle—it really offers legitimacy. Gives a frank, no-nonsense impression. It's one of the things that gave people confidence on the r/LAtruepsychics Reddit, with the notable exception of @shake_n_snake98, who thought that Valentini was perhaps fooling people by pretending he wasn't trying to fool people.

"So, Clarice, let's begin," Valentini says, finally sitting across from me, gently rolling his shoulders and straightening his spine. "Can you tell me your full name, your age, and the date and place you were born?"

"Clarice Marie Dahl. Age thirty-three. Born in New York, New York. August nine."

"Cosmopolitan. And a fire sign!"

"Well, I was born there, we left when I was twelve. We moved upstate. To a town that was decidedly not cosmopolitan."

"The names of your parents?"

"Florence Dede Sulke. Jack Allen Dahl."

"Divorced?"

"Oh, yes."

"Are you right- or left-handed?"

"Left."

"So you're weird," he says, staring at me. "Clarice, I need you to tell me exactly why you came in today. This is a place of complete nonjudgment. Your descriptions help me to feel your field and the fields of those you inquire about."

It takes me a minute to remember why it is that I'm here on Thanksgiving Day. What do I need from this man?

"I had a boyfriend a few years ago," I say, after a pause, looking at Valentini's face, his eyelids fluttering from time to time, cheeks dropped like he's sleeping, his palms surrendered upright. He nods, tells me to go on.

"We dated for just over a year, and most of the time it was chaotic. Sometimes good, sometimes really, really, really not good. At the beginning I think he was still in love with someone else, or maybe a lot of someone elses." I rub my sweaty hands on my jeans. I feel my shoulders tense. Valentini tells me to close my eyes, so I do. He lets out a long open-mouthed exhale, which I understand is a suggestion to keep talking.

"He was very secretive, and kind of a libertine, I guess? He indignantly didn't do much, or have a steady job, or much direction, or much money. He said a genius needs a lot of time to do nothing, which, you know. How to respond to that. He complained a lot, loved critical theory. I was obsessed with him. You know. Just so desperate for him to want me. I was going in and out of drinking a lot at the time. He was drinking a lot and doing drugs, mostly in private. He started having a couple of manic episodes that scared me a little. I tried to break up with him a few times, even though I was so intensely attached to him, partially because he refused to acknowledge any of his behavior was off, and partially because we weren't really happy even when it wasn't. It didn't really work. He didn't agree to it, I guess? Or he would just continue talking about how if we kept going on like this we would break up, even though I had tried to do it already. But I found out he cheated on me, and I guess I felt like that was enough of a transgression for me to have some resolve. So, I broke up with him, and then told him I didn't want him to contact me again." I open my eyes and do a few shoulder rolls, having become increasingly tense over the process of talking.

"And he didn't like that." Valentini's fingers are quickly tapping on his thighs.

"Yeah, exactly."

"Men like that never like it when their prey escapes."

"I mean, I don't know if I was his prey. Definitely his . . . well, maybe something along those lines. Yeah, I mean, he started not leaving me alone. At first it was just like, okay, he's heartbroken, I guess, or butthurt. But then it was, you know. Harassment. Calls, texts, fake numbers, fake email addresses, letters. He showed up places. Long story short, we had to go to court so I could get a restraining order. He didn't understand where I was coming from at all. I wanted him to stop talking to me, simply that, and he wouldn't do it."

"And you were living where when this happened?"

"I lived in Brooklyn at the time. I moved to LA soon after the court process ended. I've been here two years. The restraining order ran its course just last month."

"So, he's at it again?"

"Well, I'm not sure exactly."

"But you're wondering if there's still danger? Unfinished business?"

"Sort of. I was at this bar the other night, and I'm almost positive I saw him there. So I've been trying to do research to figure out if it was actually him, but I haven't been able to find out. And I don't know how without potentially putting myself in danger. Even if it's like, emotional danger, which sounds pussy, maybe—"

Valentini clears his throat, interrupting me, then says softly, "I'm going to have you close your eyes, again. Put your left hand over your heart, Clarice. Let's breathe together for a little while. Just listen to the rhythm of my breath, and if you breathe, too, we will sync."

I do as he says, close my eyes and try to inhale when I hear a quick rush into his nostrils, then exhale as he shoots it out.

When his breathing gets quieter I notice through the quick squint of my eyes that his hand rises when we exhale, lowers when we inhale. We go on like this for a while. Five, ten, fifteen minutes of breathing. The air is slightly savory. Cooking smells come through the vents from another condo. I start to fade a bit, get comfortable and sleepy on the couch, which feels like it's growing larger the longer I sit there. I begin to assume that this is all there is, that Valentini might already be doing whatever it is he does.

But he claps once, powerfully, and I startle and let out a tiny shriek. He gives no pause, just instructs me, in a noticeably deeper monotone, to "look at him deep, deeper than deep, deeper than the deepest deep." He has striking gold eyes that coruscate slightly in the candlelight and bring to mind a Brontë heroine, equal parts tortured and awestruck. I feel queasy when our gazes lock; a dizziness whacks into my head and stomach as though he hit me.

"It's okay to be uncomfortable. When we shift planes psychically we do so physically. If you need to vomit, there's a small bucket to the left-hand side of the couch," says Valentini, still looking at me, unblinking. I desperately want to close my eyes again, assuming it might pause the spin in my head, as well as the feeling of immense exhaustion, jet-lag-level exhaustion. I blink rapidly. I do have to reach for the little barf bucket, and let out one acidic heave.

He snaps his fingers at me, then slaps his palms on his thighs twice as I groan and wipe the back of my hand over my mouth, close my eyes again.

"I need you to stay here with me for a minute, Clarice. Eyes on me just a little longer. We're grounding into each other. I need you to consider the space around your body, then imagine sending your energy out, far past any distance you can imagine. We need to expand your quantum reach so I can see it clearly, we need to heighten the vibration. It's disorienting, I know that. But I need you to trust me. Do you trust me?"

"Yes?"

"Say it again, Clarice, tell your guides that you have trust in Valentini."

"Who?"

"Your spiritual guides, they're all arriving, they are landing in your field. They will help. If you trust me to be here in your field, tell them!"

"Yes! Okay!" I say, trying not to blink, trying not to barf again. "I trust you! I tru—"

"The image that is coming to me," Valentini says, cutting me off, lowering his voice considerably, "is a Doberman, a huge dog that's tied up, and is barking madly, and has been left out in the rain."

"And . . . is P.T. the Doberman?"

"I think so, Clarice, yes. That's how he registers in your field. Once a dog like this finally falls asleep, you don't want to poke him, you don't want to wake him up," Valentini emphasizes. He looks frightened, honestly.

"Meaning it's bad to find out if it's him?" I say. "Or you mean don't get in touch with him?"

"Absolutely do not." Valentini put up his hand in a stop gesture. "I see he brought to your life a kind of . . . cloud of mental ailment."

"My roommate at the time thought he was untreated bipolar?"

"I'm not here to diagnose, but I'm leaning BPD," he says. "That being said, it's not what causes this type of subconscious hellscape. Emotional regulation is a challenge, but there's something even deeper than that going on."

"What does that mean?" I ask. "Like evil?"

"I can see during your court process, he entered into many

dark fantasies. Yes, some dreams of hurting you physically. But no will to act."

"Oh, fabulous." I start taking dainty sips from the cup near my feet, which is all my stomach can handle. "What if he has the will to act now?"

"Well, at the time, he wanted to keep track of you. To control you. You went off social media?"

"For a long time. Now I have a finsta."

"Which is . . . ?"

"It's like a private account only my friends follow. The profile picture is my late childhood cat."

"Does he know what Moon looked like?"

"How did you know my cat's name was Moon?"

"That's why you came all the way to Torrance, Clarice."

"Right. I don't think he knew what Moon looked like."

"Keep this finster private nevertheless."

"So, he's still looking for me?" I start to smell a whiff of the little bucket of vomit. "Do you mind if I get some more water and maybe move that barf?"

"You stay where you are," he says, snapping his finger once in front of his face. I rub my eyes; he moves the bucket and gets me more water. Then he sits down, does another snap, and dives right back in.

"A rejection and accusation, being proved wrong, to a man like that—is not something he'll ever fully get over."

"So, I am in danger? Is he near me? Was that him that I saw?"

Valentini goes quiet again, which I assume means he's seeing my aura hurtling toward a bloody, unfortunate murder. My heart pounds, my stomach churns what's left of the McDonald's breakfast sandwich I had on the way over here.

"It's not totally clear to me," Valentini says after a while.

"Even you can't tell if it was him?"

"No, I can't. His current self is not registering as readable.

There's something protecting, and sort of blocking, the location of his field. Like rubber, a murky, impenetrable force."

"Maybe he's dead."

"He's not. They're telling me your father has a similar energy."

"My dad? Let's maybe not conflate the two, but, uh, yeah."

"Your father's ill? Convalescent?"

"Yeah, he had an aneurysm," I say. "I don't know all the details. We don't talk."

He goes quiet again for a little while; his closed eyes begin to blink like he's in REM sleep. From the darkness of the hallway beyond where he sits, a rotund calico cat makes its way into the living room and pops up onto my lap.

"Jessica is trying to calm you," he says, her claws digging into me as she makes herself comfortable on my legs. "She's very sensitive."

My eyes are still open, locked on his face, and his are still closed.

"Your father and P.T. They are of the same wound in your field. And they are present in your consciousness in a way they shouldn't be."

"Okay," I say. "So what does that mean?" I realize I'm petting Jessica rapidly now, and small tufts of fur are attaching to my black sweater. One lands on Valentini. "Does that mean I didn't see him?"

"You did see him . . . but it's difficult for me to tell if you actually saw him."

"Come again?"

"Well, as I said, his whereabouts are extremely murky to me. But I am getting the message that whether or not it was the real him is not that significant. He appeared to you, one way or another. Which means, in a metaphysical sense, and possibly a physical sense, he's around."

I rearrange myself, upsetting Jessica. She hops off my lap and curls up beneath Valentini's chair.

"Val, I am here because I want confirmation as to whether or not he's in LA, going to my local coffee shops and watching me sleep."

"Well, I can tell you, Clarice, I'm good at what I do. And he's not registering to me in an exact location on this plane. I do think he's still unwell, that much I can tell."

"Okay," I say, pinching the bridge of my nose. "Is that unusual? The not-registering-in-a-location thing?"

"Somewhat, yes." He brings his pointer finger to his lips in thought. "It happens, but it's usually because a person is in the midst of some kind of transition."

"Like moving?"

"Like moving, or traveling, or beginning a relationship."

"I swear to god if this fucking guy is in love . . ." I get a wave of exhaustion and have the impulse to ask Valentini if I can have a blanket. I deny it.

"I'm not sensing love, exactly," Valentini says. "His position with Eros is tainted. A dishonesty to it, even a personal death impulse."

"I'll say," I say.

"Listen, again, what matters most is that he appeared. He's not out of your energetic space. And he needs to be. He needs to be cast out in the same way you need to cast out your father."

"How do I do that?"

"Continue healing, for one," he says. "You can get help casting him out. I know people. There's a fabulous light healer in South Pasadena."

"Right," I say. "Maybe text me that info."

"However, if you let P.T. into your energetic space, if you allow him in again, if you ever try to reach out to him, to confront him . . ."

"Then what?"

"It's a poison. I can see it swirling around in your mind."

"Okay, but if you don't know where he is, and I don't know, how am I supposed to make sure I'm safe? How am I supposed to just let that go?"

"Let's stop talking for a moment and breathe again. I'd like to seal up the area and your field."

For about a minute, Val starts speaking under his breath, quickly. I can't make out any of the words or even what language he's speaking. I am open to this kind of thing. I came here, after all, I believe in the human capacity to know and sense beyond what we generally accept as reality. But this moment makes me wonder. The elf-speak makes me wonder.

"Another thing, Clarice, before we close entirely." Valentini opens his eyes, startling me. "I don't want to frighten you by bringing this up, but I do sense a little dark energy around your home space. Be aware of that. It might be an okay idea to move to a new place."

We sit there for a little while longer as he guides me through a closing breath sequence. I'm mad. All I get from this guy is "don't go looking for him"? The same advice I got from Roz. And neither of them can answer what I ask back: Well, what if he goes looking for me? I wanted Valentini to say that he was safely in a mental health institution somewhere in New Zealand, or perhaps that he had succumbed to a rare genetic disease. Valentini can sense my frustration.

"I know what I've told you is unclear," he says. "But I really think this is about repairing your relationship to the masculine."

We sit there looking at each other. He breaks the quiet between us and takes out a laminated Venmo sign with his scan code. We pause for a moment by the door while I send him the money.

"You *can* stop them from blocking you from romantic intimacy." Val places his hand, lightly, on my shoulder. "These men. Your father, P.T., other men who violated you or your ancestral line."

"I honestly don't have any interest in romantic intimacy."

"Maybe that can be true for some. I've been on ice since '16 myself. But it's not true for you."

"No. It is true," I say forcefully, my voice cracking a little, betraying the emotion that's been building for the whole hour.

"Seclusion is the devil you know, Clarice."

"Which would make love, what, the other devil?"

"Yes. And it's inescapable. It comes for us all."

"Sounds like a threat," I say.

He opens the door to let me out, then lifts his chin up at me, which is peppered with zit scars and a suggestion of stubble.

"Can I ask you a question before you go?" He narrows his eyes.

"Sure," I say, still sulking. I look down and for the first time, somehow, register that he's barefoot.

"Clarice. Are you named after . . . ?"

It was not what I was expecting him to ask. I give a weak nod. "I tell most people no, but yes."

"An interesting choice."

"My dad was a horror fan and she was the bravest woman he could think of."

Valentini nods, then closes the door.

11

Happy Thanksgiving doll

Wish you were here

U know that is why the wedding is on
Christmas Eve

so you must come to your mothers

where Santa can find you
-Mom

U don't have to sign ur texts

Happy Gobble

never forget the American atrocities of
this dark holiday

Oh for god sakes Clarice
-Mom

I drive from Torrance to Bunny's sister Nicole's house. She and her wife, Tiff, are hosting for Thanksgiving and of course Tiff unsuccessfully pretends she's not annoyed that I'm there a cool twenty minutes before eating—as Bunny promised me for pie preparation last night, and table setting today, which obviously I flaked on. I can't give the real excuse, so I opt for saying nothing. Tiff, Nicole's wife, is a real ship captain. Their kids aren't allowed white sugar and their schedules are planned months in advance. Tiff's one of those people whose first instinct is always to doubt outwardly, never to doubt themselves. Admirable depending on the circumstance. Tiff's the first one I see when I enter through their palatial kitchen—jade countertops, industrial stovetop, nine thousand sinks. She's stirring three different pots as a guy in a plaid bow tie and bowler hat leans against the glass-front fridge and talks about *America's Got Talent*, of all things. She's obviously not paying attention, but this guy is so uncomfortable or unaware that he doesn't notice. I smile at him barely as he quietly introduces himself as *Richard, actually, um, Rich who works with Nicole.* A bit of cracker flies out of his mouth. He quickly scuttles away. "Thank god," Tiff mouths.

"Bunny thought you were coming to help with pies," she says, becoming chilly, turning back toward a pot of gravy. "Not a big deal."

"I brought some cookies," I offer, and she pauses the spoon again, turning again to look at me, raising one brow.

"From where?"

"The Vons on Sunset and Virgil? They're open until two a.m.? Huge parking lot? You know it? Great deals on day-olds," I say, and pause with her stiffening silence before adding, "I'm kidding, Tiff, they're from Proof."

"Well, ha-ha. Put them out on the dessert table," she says, shaking her head at me but cracking a small smile. Nicole once told me that when Tiff stops being overly accommodating, like she is to guests, and starts getting mad at you, it's her way of expressing you matter to her. Next-level WASP subtext. Even though Bunny and Nicole grew up with a lot of money,

Nicole "married up," as it is defined in America. Tiff's parents are the progeny of huge corporate overlords (sugar and oil—dirty money), who themselves became prominent figures in the NYC nonprofit industrial complex. They learned how to manage "good deeds" with the same spirit for business. Vaguely friends with the Clintons and, like, Diane Sawyer. We aren't allowed to mention the Epstein plane around Tiff because once five years ago Nicole joked that maybe Tiff's dad went to Little St. James and they almost got separated.

Nicole was their parents' biological child and always defined herself as antiestablishment, as it were, meaning she listened to punk and volunteered at an LGBTQ soup kitchen into her early thirties. I used to spend most of the summer at Nicole and Bunny's parents' place during college, and though Nicole already lived in her own apartment, she frequently came over to watch soccer on the big-screen and get into political fights with her apolitical parents over a dinner prepared by the live-in housekeeper. So she and Tiff are a nice match. Together they make disparaging jokes about middle America while paying for their wood-fired oven with Pfizer stock.

After I put the cookies on the dessert table, which features fruit tarts on cake stands, multiple pies, and a chocolate fountain with skewered fruit, I go out to the garden to find Bunny. She's smoking a rollie on the wooden swing set, watching her nieces and a gaggle of other kids playing badminton. I try to make my face normal as I walk toward her, to hide the emotional fatigue from the day with Valentini. Luckily she misreads my expression.

"Bitch, I have one on holidays. Stab me," she says, sucking in deep.

"Bunny, I don't give a shit if you smoke. You give a shit if you smoke." I come to the swing set and move her purse to sit on the slide. Inside the purse, I notice, is a self-help book. It happens to be Bunny's preferred genre of literature.

"As a friend you should be concerned for my health," she says, offering the cigarette to me, though I decline.

"What's this?" I ask, picking up the book, entitled *Letting the Right One In.*

"Clarice, I don't want to hear it."

"Isn't *Letting the Right One In* the title of a horror movie?" I start flipping through it, biting my tongue at the blocks of inspirational quotes, the assignments, the goofy, cartoonish illustrations.

"Put that away or I'll put this out in your eyes," she says, holding the cig like a dart.

"What about our fair Chris? Or Crust, as I like to call him?" I say, putting my hands up in surrender.

"I already knew you call him that, by the way. But what about him? Not that he's going to be the last person I bone, but this is about releasing unconscious behaviors, what keeps us from deep connection. You should read it."

"I connect plenty," I say. "And I've had enough excitement for one day."

"Right, where have you been?" Her eyes sharpen; I can see the wheels turning. "Please don't say it had to do with P.T.?"

"No." I swallow, hopefully not too hard. This woman knows me so well. It's touching, but in this instance, uncomfortable. "I've been sleeping. You know I hate holidays."

"I know." She nods, softens, takes another drag.

"You hate holidays, Clarice?" Crust is holding two glasses of red wine and has wafted down from the back porch, where other guests are mingling with charcuterie and a hired-gun cello player.

"Thank heavens, you made it," I say quietly, so only Bunny can really hear, and she lightly smacks my arm. I stand and take one of the wines from Crust's hand just as he's handing one to Bunny. It's clearly not for me, but I watch him weigh his options and gracefully remain silent.

"Well, Chris," I say with a smile, taking a sip that warms my body, "foremost, Thanksgiving reminds me of the year my dad came at my mom with a carving knife while threatening to kidnap me and my brother, then accidentally stabbed himself in the thigh."

"Ha, right, same here!" He laughs.

"It's true, Chris," Bunny says, even though I can tell I'm annoying her.

"You've never been held hostage by your dad?" I say.

"Oh, god, I thought . . . That's horrible . . ." Crust trips over his innocent misstep, mouth agape, his cheeks gone maroon.

"You couldn't have known." I take another sip and see Bunny roll her eyes. She hates when I use traumatic tales as a party trick. I add, clearing my throat, "Tell me about your Thanksgivings."

He lets out a relieved breath. "We spend holidays at Auntie Deb's," Chris starts, "and at some point we said, fuck turkey and stuffing, we're from North Carolina, let's do a full-blown barbecue—"

Tiff rings a pineapple-shaped dinner bell and cuts him off, announcing that dinner has commenced.

"To the grub!" I bolt away from them both, particularly from Crust humanizing himself to me.

Since I came in the back, I didn't notice how many guests they'd invited. Why have a six-million-dollar home if you can't share it? It's assigned seating (names, cursive, on a corn-shaped name tag). I've been sat between Crust and the twerp from the kitchen, Rich. When you make errors in Tiff's planning, she punishes you via table placements to show she's noticed. Whoever is in her good graces gets to sit next to her favorite daughter, Frances—an easy laugh. Tonight that's Bunny and a red-haired teenager I don't recognize.

Crust looks at me, after we each get our plates, concerned. "So."

". . . So?"

"Did you want to finish that awful story about your father?" he says, clasping his hands together like he's preparing to pray. "That seems like something you might want to get off your chest."

Instead of being repulsed by his earnestness, I feel touched, also pained. I'm certainly wrong but I imagine everyone around the table, richly dressed in their linen two-piece sets and leather mules, has had a smooth past. But being raised by an abusive drunk and a love addict is more common than not, isn't it? A communal tale if there ever was one. A tired one.

"Oh, yeah," I say, breaking a roll and buttering it. It's vulgar but I lick the end of the knife, which is pewter and heavy. The butter is hand-churned by their part-time personal chef, a man named Pietro who trained as a sous chef at some impressive restaurant in Moscow. "I mean, he drunk-drove from his apartment in the city, broke into the house we had moved into upstate, and threatened to kill my mom unless she surrendered us to him," I say. "She started flipping out, but my brother, Damian, and I were so scared he would actually kill her that we ran outside and into the back of the Oldsmobile he borrowed, the driver-side door still swung open, car still on, radio still on." I bite into the roll, which has about an inch of that butter, and take a long time to chew. I enjoy having a captive audience. Chris's salad fork is standing upright in a fondant potato. "To this day I can't hear 'Alice's Restaurant' without feeling slightly suicidal."

"Did you think he would actually do it?" His eyes creased, he leans forward.

"Yeah, I was a kid," I say as he reaches over me for some champagne and fills my glass, then his. "I was worried he would kill her until it became clear he was just, I don't know. An idiot."

"God," Crust says. "Did you go back inside? Did he come and get you?"

"Damian vomited in the back seat so we went back inside. My mom was locked in the bathroom screaming, on the phone with the cops. My dad was on the couch in the fetal position, the carving knife by his shoes."

"That must have been so painful to see," says Crust, and I can tell he means what he says.

"It's okay," I say back, suddenly embarrassed. I do this sometimes. I overshare, and it gets me a little high, then I immediately feel bad. At least I don't tell Crust what I actually felt that day, when I came back inside to find my dad on the couch crying. I was ashamed of him. His madness lacked follow-through. Just how much was he able to control himself? It wasn't clear. I had this muddled notion that if he had the audacity to threaten, he better have the moxie to act. Be a man and murder your ex-wife and children.

P.T. was similarly horny to make holidays bad, no shock there. We didn't have a good one the whole year we dated but we spent them all together. Before P.T. I hadn't experienced having "someone" to bring home to Thanksgiving. He texted me he was getting in his car to drive up to my mom's place upstate after we'd already started eating. He was pissed for no discernible reason by the time he showed up and barely spoke to me or my family. I could see Damian and my mom giving each other looks. I overheard my mom and Mitch whispering in the kitchen. His attitude was particularly confusing because the day before I left, a week earlier, we'd spent all night having sex and getting pizza delivered at 3 a.m., watching TCM, laughing.

Crust, or in this particular moment, Chris, puts his hand just so on my forearm. When Rich tries to peer into our conversation, Chris says kindly, with no wink or knowing expression, "Just trying to lead another soldier onto the crypto-field!"

Not long into dinner, around the time the second course is served by cater-waiters, I figure out that Nicole is trying to set me up with Rich. She comes over, places a hand on each of our backs, and starts talking about how we both like old movies, that the three of us should go together sometime to the upcoming double features at the New Bev, then creates a text group "just so we all have each other's numbers." Nightmare. Like Bunny, Nicole has an extremely high sex drive and hasn't been single longer than a week the whole time I've known her, so my disinterest in coupledom, or polyamory, or even low-pressure casual dating, or whatever, feels truly befuddling and perhaps even frightening to her. It means that she, too, has an underlying concern for my solitude and now this poor, foolishly dressed man has been roped in.

Even before dessert, I decide to Irish goodbye. An old family friend Tiff refers to as Drunkle Skipper is standing at the head of the table behind Tiff, gripping her shoulder with one hand and a crystal tumbler of creamy liquor with the other, giving a gratitude toast that takes a sharp left turn from being thankful for his new timeshare in Aruba to how betrayed he felt when his house staff tried to unionize. His hairline is wet with product, his tie as loose as his tongue. The distraction gives me an easy path to the kitchen side door. As I head down the driveway, I see Crust outside, too, and hear him talking to someone about his client roster and the banger year they are about to have as he "makes dem some bank." It erases some of the kindness he showed me.

I drive aimlessly for a while, eventually to a Del Taco drive-thru, ask the little black speaker if anything comes without cheese, get carne asada steak fries, then immediately drive over to a trash can to get rid of them because I don't like the smell. I find a middle spot in the nearly empty parking lot, put on some music, and try to breathe. I tap on my steering wheel. I close my eyes and try to remember some of the things Valentini told me earlier that day, but it all comes to my mind as total nonsense: *Don't wake a mean sleeping dog. You aren't as lonely as you think you are. P.T. is a cloud somewhere.*

My phone vibrates. It's an off-chain text from Rich.

Off you went? So nice to meet you. Perhaps a trip to the theater . . .

I immediately erase it and place my phone in my bag. I notice Bunny has placed her ridiculous book inside it. I take it out and see a Post-it on it that says: *The horror movie was called "LET" the Right One In. This is "Letting" the Right One In. GFYS. ILY. xxx B*

I toss it in the back of my car and redownload Instagram. To my alarm, P.T. has posted something. An old cartoon with a bunch of turkeys standing on an elephant that says: *Don't let the turkeys get you down.* That's it. No caption, thirteen likes. I search through the likes and look at all of the likers' profiles. None provide clues. An hour passes before I realize it, and by the time I erase Instagram again, I feel a thick grief spinning through me. Being an obsessive person is physically painful like that. You're sucked into a whirlpool of dark energy. There's not much I can do when I get in this state. I leave the planet, any sense of wisdom or clarity evaporates and is replaced by mind hunger. Once Roz referred to it as lost time, but I started crying when she said that, so she quickly backtracked and reframed. If being trapped by fear or obsession means I've lost time, I've lost more than half my life. Even when I was with P.T. I was still doing "research," trying to catch him in lies and prevent myself from being hurt. The crux of course being that I was in pain virtually all the time, in a constant state of readiness for total disaster.

Hovering right above the Del Taco is one of those ubiquitous billboards for an LA personal injury firm that reads: "WHO HURT YOU?" It's completely dark now, except for the considerable brightness of the LED poles. I've sat here in a fast-food parking lot for that long. *You hate holidays, Clarice?* I left a place I was welcome because I'd rather be nowhere, alone, anonymous and blank. And in truth, I feel at ease at fast-food places. I think most kids of divorce do—it's a secure attachment. Always here, always the same. Not the first Thanksgiving I've spent at one. I wonder how many others are sitting in parking lots like this, or having a clandestine cigarette in a garage, trying to escape the claustrophobic expectation to be somewhere, enjoying togetherness. There's only so much of that some of us can take.

12

The first time I saw P.T. since our encounter outside my apartment was in court. Maxine came with me again, in downtown Brooklyn, on Joralemon Street. She brought along her sister's eight-month-old daughter, whom she had tucked in a BabyBjörn. She said she thought a nearby baby would work well for my image. I was concerned she thought my image needed working.

"A baby who doesn't belong to either of us?" I said as we stood in the cold.

"You think that judge is gonna be questioning this baby?" she said back, bouncing the kid and fixing her hat, knit to resemble a strawberry. I had slept not at all the night before, save for one hour around 6 a.m. where I dreamed of whales covered in oil washed up on a beach, dead. I looked and felt like a well-fed ghost. Maxine had left early to get the baby but texted me not to leave the house without brushing my hair and putting on foundation and an "I-made-some-effort outfit." I was in a wool sweater with my hair brushed into a ponytail. I had thought I successfully covered my acne with some tinted sunscreen. Still, Maxine let out a judgmental exhale when she gave me a once-over outside the courthouse. That time I put my hand up in a "stop" gesture before she could comment. She let it rest.

I was hoping P.T. wouldn't show up that day. That perhaps he never got the papers that the sheriff served to him, and that he had simply stopped reaching out to me through his own volition, not because of the threat of arrest. I chose to ignore the fact that the precinct had left me a voicemail, telling me they delivered it to him.

The moment we walked inside, I saw P.T. standing in the security line. Wearing a suit jacket I'd gotten for him from Target so that he could accompany me to a wedding the previous May. He'd had what seemed like a mild manic episode that morning, but I didn't really know what was going on. He had talked a mile a minute about the deep state and had spent two hundred dollars getting snacks, beer, cartons of menthol cigarettes (he had quit smoking months before, and when he was smoking, he hand-rolled), and cleaning supplies (he didn't clean) at the bodega down the street from his apartment. He had refused to go on the subway to get to the wedding venue in Red Hook—it was too beautiful out, he said, plus he had sensed something "off and potentially dangerous" about the MTA that day. So we walked from Bed-Stuy. I thought it might tire him out. It took us nearly two hours and we missed half the ceremony.

But there he was, in the security line, hair slicked back like a twenties gangster, in that cheap black suit coat with jeans. He turned toward us like he sensed my presence and I went numb. I saw Maxine narrow her eyes at him and she took a dramatic step in front of me, obscuring his view with her body and her niece.

"You want to wait, Clarice? Go back outside?"

"It's fine," I said, "he's almost through."

Of course he set off the alarm a few times as he went in, getting more and more flustered, pulling up his too-large pants after removing his belt. I kept my eyes on the floor.

What must have been hours before the sheriff delivered the papers to him, I had received one more message from him. A video attached to a blank email with the subject line "MISSTER MISS HER." It was a close-up of his face as he walked down a hallway in his apartment building. His eyes shot, skin gray.

"Do you know how much I miss you? How much you hurt me?" he whispered into the camera. The sight of his lips that close up, chapped with the slightest gathering of saliva at the corners, made me gag a little.

When I forwarded Damian the message, he asked me to tell him a good memory of P.T.—he couldn't believe one person could be so unlikable. Immediately, I thought of how P.T. was when I was depressed. The times when I would sleep until late into the afternoon or wake up in the middle of the night heaving sobs. He'd just hold me tightly and pet my hair, telling me that all brilliant people have this type of immovable despair, he'd have been worried if I didn't. *Life is war, Clarice! It's structured to destroy us.* He'd bring me ice cream in bed, make me buttered noodles, and watch TV with me on my laptop. In some way, it made me enjoy these spells of depression. He respected melancholia completely.

Instead I told Damian that he could be funny sometimes, and often had beautiful epiphanies about life. Damian said psychotic people have epiphanies all the time.

"Just think about those prophets on the subway screaming in your face," Damian said. "They're mentally departed, and you don't want to date one, probably, but they're rarely wrong."

I saw mostly women sitting outside the other courtrooms. Across from us, a mother held the hands of her young kids, close in age, who were sucking on Go-Gurts. It could be worse, I thought. We could have had back-to-back kids, bound for the rest of our lives through offspring.

He wasn't outside the courtroom where we were assigned. But once we sat down on one of the rows of benches, he appeared from around the corner and sat directly behind us. I could hear him breathing, moving around. He had brought a *New Yorker* with him. He'd pick it up, then thwack it down. He walked in front of us to get some water a few times. It reminded me of a lion, swishing its tail, staking territory.

"You want to move?" Maxine said. "He's trying to get your attention."

I said no, I didn't. Anywhere else I would have had to look at him. It would have been worse. I told Maxine I needed to go to the bathroom. She said to go and she'd make sure he stayed fucking put. I went in and washed my face, then just sat on the toilet for a while looking up disturbing stuff on my phone. Particularly an article from *Psychology Today* that confirmed and communicated everything I should not have been thinking about at this moment: that nearly all male murderers claim that: (a) they committed the murder out of love and (b) it was a result of loving *too much*. The article even started with the famous O. J. Simpson quote: "Let's say I committed this crime. Even if I did do this, it would have to have been because I loved her very much, right?"

Too much love. Part of me got it, you know, feelings are overwhelming. It's horrible that other people won't stick to your designs, do what you want them to do.

I went out and sat back down. Maxine put her hand on my shoulder.

"What the hell are those?"

She was looking down at the hideous men's dress shoes I was wearing as though they were threatening her.

"Oh, I know," I said, crossing my feet and trying to move them under the pew out of her sight. "They're Clarks. From when I used to cater-waiter."

"Nope. No."

"All my other shoes are too casual!"

Maxine opened her mouth to protest, but just then, our

names were called. Together, P.T., Maxine, the little baby, and I marched solemnly into a courtroom, behind an appropriately expressionless security guard, this time a bald white guy, muscles so big he looked inflated. We sat down at tables on either side of the judge, facing her. It was Judy again.

Judge Judy, whose oil-painted portrait was looming behind her, a new addition since the last time we were there, asked me to explain what had brought me there, and like the first time, I went through it again. I had printed out his emails, our text exchanges. I handed them to a court officer, who handed them to the judge. I felt myself teetering on complete dissociation, spirit hovering just above me, drinking from a bottle of cheap, astringent liquor. I must have sounded annoyed, as though the judge should have remembered my story, because she, too, seemed bothered, and I heard Maxine cough with intention behind me. It was his presence. Him, nearby, mumbling a little, tapping his foot, rustling papers, trying to get me to look at him. I willed myself not to. Instead I kept a tight grip on the table in front of me, the finish worn down only on the edge, where others had obviously held on for dear life, too.

I could hear him sighing after I spoke, saying it wasn't true, everything I was claiming was incorrect, misinterpreted. That I was wrong, lying, simply afraid. He was trying to have a simple conversation with me, and to ask me out on a date, to begin again, that was all. My head started hurting immensely as he spoke. I was honestly confused. He wasn't saying what I expected him to say: I expected him to categorize our communications as misunderstanding and heartbreak, that he was so sorry and it would not happen again. Even if it wasn't true, it would be the way out, the way to make him seem sane.

"I love her, Your Honor. I was contacting her to get my stuff back, for one, but I also wanted her back," he said. "All of her. I wanted her to know why I did what I did. Yes, I crossed the line. My worst offense was showing up at her house. When I was seen near her work, I was at a museum and went to the crepe place across from her work because it's very delicious. I sent her some gifts, yes. Some emails, sure. I wanted to get her to talk to me. That's all."

She asked him if there was anything else he wanted to say.

"She's afraid because her dad was abusive, Your Honor. Her dad used to threaten to kill her mother. He abused her, too, I won't go into it. It's terrible, Your Honor. She's been through so much. So I can understand why she would feel scared, but I'm here to tell you that's not me. There's no reason to be afraid."

He turned to look at me again. I started shaking slightly. The guard snapped his fingers at P.T. and told him to face forward. The judge's expression was inscrutable. After a moment of riffling through the papers, she looked up at me.

"What would you like to do, ma'am? How would you like to move forward?" She went on. "In order to get a long-term order, we need to go to trial. You can petition today for a short-term order to give yourself three months, you can drop it altogether, or you can decide to go to trial to obtain a longer-term order."

I stood there for what felt like a long time, but it was probably three minutes. Minutes are long, though, a lot can occur in each one. I heard P.T. whisper, "Don't do this."

It was lonely, hearing him say all that. I'd had this guy so deep inside me my shit smelled like his morning breath, and yet I could not, in that moment, have felt more uncertain of who he was. I'd never felt so fully disconnected from him, certain that we barely knew each other. I could have been anyone to him. He could have been anyone to me, too, as long as he wanted me and withheld from me with such an adept push and pull. Were any of my feelings ever real? Was I rewriting history to deny I ever loved him because of how it turned out? Is it love if it does more harm than good in the end? What the hell had we experienced? I finally turned my head toward him. When I did, he looked away.

"Extend it. Does it really sound like he's going to leave you alone?" Maxine stood up from behind me in the rows, and I turned toward her. I looked at her baby niece's sleeping, fuzzy head and wondered what she would do, years from now, if she were in my position.

"Ma'am?" the judge prodded. I rubbed my face.

As Maxine kept saying to me, as Bunny kept saying, every time a murder happens, a shooting, people look back and piece together everything that made itself "glaringly obvious." If only someone heeded the warnings. It's fucked, but that's where the mind goes. Maybe he wasn't that dangerous, he probably wasn't, I was almost positive he wasn't. But maybe he was.

I did think the possibility of arrest would continue to give him great pause, if not stop him completely. He had a profound distrust of the police because of their ruthlessness, he said, which sometimes seemed performative, considering he wasn't their typical target. Perhaps he made himself one by giving off a certain innate sketchiness. He was a lingerer, a person who didn't look you in the eye when you spoke, often looked behind himself when walking on the sidewalk as though he'd be caught for shoplifting from a CVS at any moment. This energy was, in part, what made him alluring to me. Familiar, at least. But P.T. had spent a few nights "in the tombs," as he called jail, and told me he'd do anything not to have to go back there. Like white kids of the middle and upper class tend to do, his reports of these experiences often seemed dramatized. His lockups were for minor offenses. A DUI, a third open-bottle citation, a bar fight with a bartender. But he assured me he was serious about his deep fear of prison, and he was certain that cops had it out for him. If I removed that barrier, he would have no reason not to contact me. It made his unpredictability factor skyrocket. It's the not knowing that gets you.

"I'd like to extend it, at least for the short term," I said quietly. The judge said that on the basis of what she'd heard, she would grant the extension. Maxine let out a celebratory, slightly inappropriate cheer. But the noise P.T. made upon hearing her decision. I really can't describe it.

13

The depression that followed that day in court was almost magnificent in its depth. It started to congeal my blood. I got laid off from my office job at the creative agency a few weeks after that court date. I didn't wonder why. I had been calling out sick weekly at that point. I had also stopped remembering to do my minimal administrative duties and instead read internet trash and ate all the snacks in the kitchen. It was late February, a rough time in New York.

My direct supervisor, Tim, set me up with a remote temp job doing color correction on labels for a dog food company his sister owned, something he orchestrated after hours, through his personal email, and told me to keep it on the DL. Technically it was a step up from what I had been doing at the office, since I would actually have tasks that leaned toward being creative. *You're smart and talented, Clarice. Don't waste it on another mindless job.*

I felt his words as a dull jab. Must everyone get a boner for their career? You can't take it with you, and most of the time, whatever people are so stressed out about doing and doing so well is in the service of something pointless at best and detrimental to societal well-being at worst. We all got the memo about being a cog in the wretched wheel of the billionaires, no? Like, take a breather. Anyway, it was clear Tim felt sorry for me. At one point, before I dressed in only oversized hoodies and let my acne freely do its bidding, he'd held a small flame for me. Perhaps I imagined it, but his sorry glances seemed to communicate that he could sense there had once been chutzpah in me, a real life force, it was just obscured by emotional chaos and a diet devoid of substantial nutrition.

Working for WoofChomps was a gift. I should have sent roses to Tim. I could work from bed for the first time in my life, which is where I would have been anyway. I usually signed on to my morning meeting, fell back asleep, got up and had a trough of cereal, answered an email or two, worked an hour on an assignment they thought would take me all week, and then watched reality TV. Around four or five I would order a burrito or a slice of cake. Sometimes I would walk to pick that food up, but rarely. Whenever I had a gust of energy, I intensely cleaned the kitchen. My job meant I wasn't broke, which would have cast an even gnarlier shadow on my life. I created a modest surplus in fact—I somehow made more than I had at the Manhattan agency and only spent my money on rent and books and takeout. It made me feel like I could make a run for it, if I needed to. And had the energy. It was around then that I started dreaming about moving to LA. The weather in New York was so gray, and Bunny kept sending me pictures of goofy strangers at the public pool. *This could be us, bish.*

For months, my days did not change much. Maxine told me she was getting concerned.

"You're making too many jokes about suicide," Maxine said one morning while I mixed Cinnamon Toast Crunch with granola. "The next time you make one, I'm calling an ambulance."

"Does that mean you won't pick me up some Tylenol and Drano at the market?"

She shook her head as she stamped espresso down in a portafilter. She'd recently gotten an over-the-top machine.

"I'm gonna say something you're not gonna like."

"Shoot."

"You need a god."

"I'd love one," I said, heading back into my room.

Instead I looked for a therapist, and very briefly went to a social worker at NYU. She had me fill out this novel of a questionnaire as well as the ACE (Adverse Childhood Experience) test. Questions like:

Before your 18th birthday, did a parent or other adult in the household often or very often . . . push, grab, slap, or throw something at you?

or

ever hit you so hard that you had marks or were injured?

I got an eight out of ten. Not to brag. When I handed it to her, she sucked in air through her teeth. She told me to write down examples of these incidents and bring them to our next session. I forgot to do it, so I made a small list on some old receipts in the waiting room.

"How do you think you might categorize the behavior you describe from your father and grandfather in here . . ."

My heart started beating hard.

I was still at the point mentally where I was trying to focus on the good aspects of my dad, his creativity, his knack for storytelling, his ability to find beauty in strange places. The years we lived in Chelsea had a fantastical element to them even when our home life was horrible. I remember this time in varying shades of clarity, but since my mom worked more, we were with my dad much of the time. The building we lived in felt like an industrial labyrinth of weird creatives—Damian and I used to make little parachutes to send down the stairwells and ride the freight elevator to visit a never-ending basement where there were run-down, always filled practice spaces for dancers or musicians. We'd climb on ugly concrete sculptures while the other tenants sat and smoked and talked intensely about, who knows, openings, the Knicks, Princess Diana? Many of them probably were or became important artists, but we knew them as quiet Donelle, the guy who made sculptures of dicks with wings, or Joan, that bitch who didn't cast Dad in her shitty play at MTC.

Dad let me skip school sometimes to go to voice-over auditions with him, or watch him rehearse off-off-off-off-Broadway shows with names like *Midnight Confidential* and *Red Milk Saturday*. During the summer—at least during the weeks he wasn't on a bender and fusing his body with the couch—he brought us both to consignment stores in search of secondhand designer blazers, the library to cool off with some photo books, the Whitney. He had random friends everywhere—at newsstands, sitting on the stoops we passed, in delis. There were days when we sat in parks with hoagies (him always with a Styrofoam cup of Diet Coke and a nip of liquor) while he talked at us. His favorite topic was how art wasn't really art—life was art. *Real artists don't make art, they live. They mold and fabricate life as they like it to be.* The classic view of those who can't, is what Damian says now. But I honestly like that idea.

One of Dad's most marked characteristics was that he could not handle the expectations that came along with situations that were supposed to be pleasant. He threw my mom's layered birthday cake, something he'd spent hours making, against the fridge before we could eat it, simply because she took a phone call from a friend after dinner. He passed out watching porn the night Damian had a saxophone solo at his school concert. One year the Christmas presents were soaked in gin piss because he woke up in the middle of the night and took a wrong turn—then he complained to us about how much money had been spent for nothing.

Not surprisingly he thought getting a job of any kind other than acting was giving up. He'd make like two hundred a week doing some show, then file for unemployment and food stamps while my mom worked a diverse collection of odd jobs when she wasn't booking shows or print ads, and he'd berate her for becoming a capitalist. There was a picture of him framed in the bathroom as a teenager, his whole extended Midwestern family, grouped together smiling, and he's in the back row, giving the camera the finger.

I always tried to keep him happy when I sensed him shift from day to evening. I think most kids of alcoholics become clairsentient that way. I told him jokes, asked him to tell me stories, even to perform for me. I'd sit on the living room floor and he'd recite something. His go-tos were *Hamlet* and this disturbing poem he loved, "The Cremation of Sam McGee," about a man burning himself alive to avoid the Arctic winter. *There are strange things done in the midnight sun.* He'd hold an invisible skull of Yorick, then spin his forearm around, letting it swing down, back and forth, as if broken. I'd genuinely lose it with these flourishes, partially because he was funny, and partially because I felt an immense relief, as if an anchor had been snipped from my ankle and I could move around again. His temper, a specter, had left the room. I would clap for him; he'd teach me the words. He was a good actor, or so I thought, and so other people told me later on. Even my mother. *He could really transcend*, she told me. *When I watched him onstage, I felt my whole body light up.*

I used the tactic of becoming his audience frequently during the swaths of time when he didn't have a show going on, days that became more and more frequent as he burned more bridges in the downtown theater community. Things got worse when my mother started getting more shows or modeling gigs than he did, a dynamic that used to be flipped. He took it out on her, so eventually she quit. Small arguments would escalate. *You arrogant cunt.*

Yet the man was funny, when he wasn't being a ghoul; maybe he still is. He was also the person who imprinted the way of the homebody into my lifestyle. We barely spoke after I was a teenager, and now we don't at all, but I dared to think he would be proud that I had found a way to make money on my computer from home, sleeping as late as I liked, not ever having to put on shoes. Not that I was sure he knew what I did for a living. I also thought he probably never got sober because nothing he'd experienced felt more appealing than being buzzed with a cig and some salted nuts. His feet up, a movie on. He always said, *The greatest thing to do is not a fucking thing*, which is a sentiment I've also heard expressed in yoga classes. I felt a kinship with him in that way, as someone who would rather be on a couch wrapped in a blanket than just about anywhere else. Watching, spacing out, forgetting.

At the end of our session that day, the social worker at NYU booked me in weekly. She did so with such poorly veiled insistence it made me suspect most of her previous patients had spoken only of things like sibling rivalry, panic attacks, slowly budding porn addiction. She had some meat with me, out came the fangs. I told her I'd see her soon. Then I blocked the number from the office, never showed up again.

14

I pass out immediately after I get home from Thanksgiving at Nicole and Tiff's. The first time I've slept soundly in days. I wake up around noon the next day, take a shower hot enough to scald my shoulders, and just as I get out, I hear something. A shuffling and thump outside my door, someone's feet running down the hall, and I know, I know, I know, I know that it's him. I rush to put on my robe and throw open the door, but the culprit is gone, too quick for me. I step out of my door, and immediately into a small pile of rotten fruit and other pieces of trash.

HEY Courtney.

So, what is the word on the cameras?

Oh shit, I forgot to ask :>\

I got more "surprises" outside my door.

Is there someone else in management

I can chat with?

Of course, no response to that. I decide to just bite the bullet and order a little door camera online. I then spend the next twenty minutes going through each piece of trash, feeling like something might give me proof it's from P.T., but it's all classic stuff, nothing particularly incriminating. Fruit (two squeezed lemons, two apple cores, a few small strawberries), a Jollibee mango-pineapple pie wrapper, a can of Coke.

I shovel everything into a bag to bring it down past the laundry room into the back alley, wondering if I should keep the Coke can and how much it would cost to get a DNA test. I remember saving a lock of his hair in a locket at one point—did I remember to get rid of that? I get out there, start to heave the bag into the bin, and hear a woman's small, soft voice yell out "No!" just as the door shuts behind me.

"Oh, fuck," I say, looking over at who I now see is Screaming Bird Girl. I take in her expression of defeat, along with the fat joint she's got in the corner of her mouth. True lovers of the devil's lettuce, this Bird couple. "We're locked out here, aren't we?"

"Mmm-hmm," she says. "And I don't even have my phone."

"Yeah, neither do I. Distracted," I say. "How long have you been out here?"

She looks a bit dazed and bounces her shoulders up and down once. "A while," she says. "I'm not sure."

"Is, your, um, boyfriend—"

"No, he didn't do this." She shakes her head gruffly and avoids eye contact.

"No, I wasn't going to say that." I half lift my hands in surrender. "I was going to ask if he was home."

"No," she says. "I don't think so. He left a while ago. I'm not sure where."

I nod. Again it occurs to me that perhaps it is one of the Screaming Birds, maybe this Screaming Bird, who leaves these "gifts" at my door. I have announced myself as a witness, after all. Maybe it's a warning to keep to myself.

There's no way to walk to the front of the building from the back alley, so for a minute I try to think about scaling the fence, but this being East Hollywood, it's not only too tall, but around the back half near the garbage there are some small rings of barbed wire at the top. When they put it up a few months ago, Courtney sent an email about it, saying that we did not have to worry that they were putting up these unsightly safety measures, it was because of racoons, not because we were in danger from "mentally ill and addicted unhoused neighbors." Then a rumor circulated throughout the building, which I heard about while doing laundry, that some drunk guy tried to break into one of the ground-floor apartments. I live on the ground floor. I now entertain the idea that it might have been a crazed P.T.

"You put it in the wrong one, by the way," Screaming Bird Girl says, and I shoot her a look, unsure of what she's talking about.

"Your trash. That big blue one is trash, the green one is recycling," she says, bringing her hand very close to her face and pointing a finger.

"Oh, no shit," I say. "I thought blue indicated recycling."

"I know, it does for smaller bins, these are just dumpsters. Courtney never told me either, I just figured it out. Well, some other woman had to tell me last time I was here. I'm really an airhead."

"Well, thanks for sharing," I say. "I guess I am, too."

I stand there awkwardly for a moment, then decide to take a seat where she is, a few strides away from the bins.

"You know this basement guy here, who lives underneath me?" I say, lifting my chin up toward the little window of his, where I see a dying plant in the window. "Do you think maybe he's in there?"

"I don't think he likes being disturbed," she says. "Because yes he is in there, and I sort of tried to knock on that little window with that curtain rod someone threw out, and he didn't answer."

"Are you sure he heard you?"

"I do think so, yes."

I don't believe her, I can barely hear her now, so I hoist

myself up on an old can of paint, take the same curtain rod, and start to bang. I can partially see into the kitchen. In fact, I can see the top of a balding head duck out of sight, behind a fridge.

"Dude, I saw you moving. Just open the door!" I scream. Nothing, no response. I give the little window one more slam of the stick.

"How did we get tasked with these neighbors? Everyone is unhinged or a hermit." I jump off the chair, toss the rod, and slide down the wall again, next to Screaming Bird Girl. She taps her shoes, off-brand Keds-type sneakers, shiny, unmarked white, peeking out from a billowing hippie skirt. We sit there in the thick stink of trash and marijuana, my sciatica starting to act up almost instantly from the unforgiving concrete.

"So," I say after a while. "Where are you from?"

"Who, me?"

"Well . . . yeah," I say, raising a brow. A small breeze causes the garbage-rot smell to come at us even harder, thick and unrelenting.

"I grew up on the Gold Coast in Chicago. My parents own a few apartment buildings there."

"Oh, no kidding." I watch a rope of smoke rise from the joint into the air.

It's fucked up and classist of me, considering I live where she lives and I was the person in P.T.'s building screaming like she and her boyfriend scream just a handful of years ago, but I figured she was going to tell me she grew up in Appalachia or in the parking lot behind a Denny's. That she met the Screaming Bird Guy because they were reselling Snickers on the same block.

"Are you wondering why I live here?" She drags out "here" like she's taunting me, like she knows exactly what I'm thinking. I've never spoken at length with someone who has a voice this nebulous, like the words have no edges. I try to remember what it sounds like when she's yelling and I can't.

"No, no. I mean, I live in this place." I try to smile.

"I got an abortion a few years ago and my family is Orthodox. I don't get any kind of support from them. Maybe most people don't at twenty-three," she says. Thank god she's not looking at me because my eyes widen. I thought she was older than me. She's concentrating hard on the sky, so I follow her gaze up there. There's a plane going over us. A few long moments go by, gravid with silence.

"Has anyone left random stuff outside your door?" I ask suddenly, wanting to say something, anything.

"I got 4G's package the other day," she says, clearing her throat a little, volume raising slightly. "I opened it by accident, it was one of those hammocks for cats."

"Yeah, no, I meant things a little weirder. I've been getting these odd objects left outside my door. Some used Q-tips. A book. Vague notes. And just now, the trash I brought out—that was spilled in front of my door."

"Are you asking if I did it?" Her eyes broadcast both defense and earnest concern. She brings it up so quickly. It makes me think it's equally possible that she absolutely did or did not do it. Either way, the speed with which she answers is very indicative of living a life on guard.

"No, how would you have?" I say. "You've been stuck out here."

"I know," she says. "Do you think someone is doing it on purpose?"

"Yeah, I mean, I can't imagine the Q-tips were a mistake. Or the binoculars."

"Why would someone leave binoculars?"

"I think it was supposed to be symbolically threatening. *I'm watching.*"

"That's so odd," she says, thinking. "Do you think maybe it's Courtney?"

"Courtney, our building manager?" I rearrange myself on

the concrete, trying to find some position where the trash stench is a little less severe. "No, that hadn't occurred to me. And I don't think it's anyone in the building."

"Do you have any ideas, then?" she asks.

I open then close my mouth. She can't be that judgmental. She has the complexion of a pile of ash, seemingly the strength of a Beanie Baby, a publicly toxic relationship. It might be helpful to her; sharing my own past troubles with a man might make her more inclined to trust me. *We don't love these guys despite them being assholes*, I'll tell her. *We love them because they're assholes! These are the subtle powers of self-hatred.*

"I had this boyfriend-turned-harasser a while back and I saw him a couple weeks ago in a bar; he's not even supposed to live here. And that's more or less the same time I started finding all this stuff at my door."

Screaming Bird Girl has taken out a Bic from the pocket of her patchwork zip-up, relighting her joint. She lifts it toward me. I decline with a smile.

"What will you do if you see him again?"

"I'm not entirely sure."

"Well, have you thought about calling him?"

"No, definitely not," I say. "I also don't have his number anymore."

She pauses for a moment, takes a dorm-life-sized hit. "So, you think he's leaving these things as a way to tell you he still wants you?"

"By leaving me trash?"

"Well, I don't know. I guess I was thinking of it like negging or something? You know guys."

"I guess."

"You think he's threatening you?"

"Uh, yes. That's the fear, yeah."

"I'm sorry," she says, and I'm not sure if she means it.

"Yeah," I say.

"Love is so hard."

"Yeah," I say again.

"Maybe, um, this is not the best thing to say. But I would have trouble not giving in if Robbie—that's my boyfriend—if he was looking for me. Especially after all that time. Honestly, I would probably feel sad if he didn't put in that much effort. I'd have a sense of what I meant to him. To still look for someone two years later?" Her voice lilts. I realize I'm witnessing the verbal deluge of her high. It makes me want to stop her from sharing her thoughts—it's blatantly out of character. I opened an emotional door here and now she's mistaken me for someone she actually knows. "People have so many ways of showing true feelings. It's some kind of effort to get your attention. Because he doesn't know how to tell you how much you mean to him."

"Well, hmm. Yeah, to get my attention, sure, maybe. Not sure it's indicative of his caring for me," I say. "It didn't, or doesn't, feel like it has much to do with me at all, after a point. Our breakup happened to be the place he directed his mental episode. His feelings were more important than what I wanted."

"Which was what?"

"To be left alone."

"Right. It's hard," she says again, holding back a cough. "For people to let go."

"Sure," I say, annoyed now. Right. I could have let P.T. apologize to me once more, and then once more after that. I could have let it be, maybe seen how far he would have gone. Skulking around and calling and sending gifts isn't all that bad. Maybe I wasted my own time and energy out of paranoia.

"I know that my parents, I mean, my father always made gestures toward my mother that would not be accepted nowadays," Screaming Bird Girl says, not clocking my irritation. "He was very insistent. When they first met, she was a teenager. He asked her out at the movie theater where she worked but she declined.

Then he secretly followed her home one night, then waited outside her apartment every day until she agreed to go on a date with him. He begged on his knees. He thought it was romantic. Her whole family thought it was romantic."

"That's an intense, uh, gesture, yeah," I say. Part of me gets it. That despite all of this, maybe I, too, would want for a handsome stranger to fall in love with me one day, so immediately and intensely. The only kind of romance that could entice me from this abstinence would be raging and impossible to stop. Insistence, persistence. Cinematic, a little terrifying. The other part thinks that the description of her dad offers some clue as to why she's living with a guy who loudly, unabashedly, threatens to kill her.

"I'm a feminist and stuff but men are not allowed to express lust or desire anymore. Men are afraid to be too up-front with women. And I'm shy, so if Robbie hadn't hit on me really obviously like he did, we wouldn't be together." She moves herself to face me ever so slightly more.

"Yeah, I mean, sure. People probably have a little more trepidation with their desire nowadays." I lick my lips, which are very dry. "Not sure that's exactly the theme of *my* situation, though. He was pretty forthright. Pretty expressive about what he did or did not want."

"Hmm." Her expression is inscrutable.

"And your dad's loitering was romantic to your mom because she liked it, right? Because if she didn't want it, it would have just been a creepy dude following her home and waiting outside her building." Or maybe she didn't know what she wanted, I want to add but don't. Maybe she didn't think to ask herself.

"You know, I don't know if she really liked it or not," she says, rasping a bit. She finishes a drag, then coughs for a good ten seconds, her face turning a dark shade. I wait for her to continue. "My dad knew the doorman in her building and he introduced him to my grandparents. They just really wanted her to get married and he had money. My mom has been irritated with him for as long as I can remember, so maybe she didn't like it after all. Anyway, I do think Robbie would do that same stuff if I left him, what you're saying. He wouldn't leave me alone until I came back to him. But you think that's a bad thing."

"I don't even know you guys," I say, reddening.

"Well, that's true. No one here really knows us. And we're fine with that." She takes one last hit of the jay, flicks off the burning end, twists it, then puts the small remainder back in her pocket. "We're kind of loners. But I don't necessarily believe what people say about healthy relationships. There was a while when Robbie and I would fight all the time and I thought it was really unhealthy. Then I realized—we are so honest with each other. We show each other every part, everything ugly. Fuck people thinking it's supposed to be all nice!" she says as she takes out the clip in her hair and aggressively redoes her bun. Admittedly she gives off an unsettling energy. It's clear, as she gives her two cents on lover's quarrels, that she does, in fact, remember that I offered her help that day. She feels indignant or embarrassed, it's hard to tell. So do I.

"I had to come to terms with a man like Robbie being what I need. It's better to be with someone even if he brings you to the edge. You want to be challenged. I believe in karma, not like punishment, but like we learn lessons through each other. We wouldn't be together if we weren't supposed to be. Do you think that kind of thing is true?"

"Sometimes I do." I nod, trying to neutralize my expression against any rising discomfort that could distort it, because I think she sounds deluded. Even a little stupid. But I relate to her—very much. The lens of disdain, I suppose, is recognizing myself. You spot it, you got it, they say. She could be reading from a journal entry I wrote about P.T. way back when. Other people are teaching us things about ourselves all the time. It's unmerciful, but I feel like something spiritually essential has been taken from Screaming Bird Girl—Robbie juiced her figurative fruit and drank it. Life force drained by the hour. You can watch that happen to a person and be powerless to stop it. I am getting a glimpse of how my friends and family saw me.

Generally when people witness a bad relationship, they hold their tongues in the moment and talk shit from the sidelines. After it ends horribly, they say it isn't your fault. But I'm pretty sure most people think what I'm thinking right now. Even subconsciously, or with guilt. That you're a little bit of an idiot. You're sick and giving off a smell. You're completely ignorant as to what love really is. I've done it, it's been me, I had no control, I was utterly obligated to someone, but still. I have some primal awareness of—and revulsion for—her weakness. To separate yourself from the weakness, internally, as a bystander, feels good.

When we first started dating, P.T. texted me that quote attributed to Plato, "Love is a grave mental disease." I swooned, even let out a giggle that he used the word "love." He followed it up with a text that read: *fucked but correct.* I remembered that quote sometimes when things were unbearable with him, a perverted affirmation. When I started to realize that what P.T. and I had was not particularly good for me, it made me grip on even tighter. That's the humbling pill to swallow. My instinct was to mop up the mess secretly instead of making an escape. In part because I felt his love—so powerful and hard to come by—could fix what felt deeply wrong with me.

During the court process I remember wanting to think any human animal could fall into a situation like the one I fell into with P.T., like Screaming Bird Girl is in with Robbie. With someone who turned out to be scary, and probably showed you, at least in little ways, they were scary all along. But I don't know if that's true. There are people out there who know how they should be treated, and in fact find it strange when people like us find ourselves in such bad company. It's not logical, the pull toward a person who's somehow dangerous. Obviously. If it doesn't intrinsically make sense, it never will. Even now, when I consider my fear of him—sure, there's the idea that he might crawl into my bedroom and slit me down the middle like a hunted duck, ripping out a still-beating heart. But many of my actual dead-of-sleep nightmares about P.T. are that we get back together and I have to explain this choice to my family and friends.

Screaming Bird Girl is here defending her own choices. She's telling me that someone's demands, someone's threats or loss of control—that might just be the fullest expression of love. And I know cognitively that's wrong after all the therapy I've been through, but at my core I believe that same thing to be true. Relational transgression, that's intimacy, that's the meat of true love. Siphoning energy out of each other until some nihilistic cloud takes the place of your soul for a while—that's the by-product of loving each other. Tearing your own clothes off in jealous rage, threatening suicide, packing a bag and putting your shoes on to leave but not leaving—passion. Eating a simple dinner after fighting like rabid dogs—tenderness. So much of love is whatever horrible shit only the two of you know. You mistake that for loyalty, living through what you don't want. Enduring is the work.

I've said to Roz before that I believe the problem-solving part of my mind died as a reaction to witnessing and experiencing so much violence as a kid. It went dim. I'm imagining deadened, once-pink flesh. It's been proven that repeated childhood trauma alters your neural pathways and affects healthy development, which is a diplomatic way of saying it gives you brain damage. Will I ever meditate enough to successfully create more positive neural connections? Hard to say. Roz told me to go to this childhood abuse survivors group when we first started working together, I guess to get me out of this kind of negative, hopeless thinking. Six women on chairs in a basement with coffee and Royal Dansk, like an AA meeting. Led by a couple of girls in their late twenties getting their clinical hours in. It was humbling to look at everyone, thinking they were losers, then realize I was a part of the group. I immediately hated every face, and they probably hated me, too. Or not, which would feel somehow more humiliating. The clinicians asked us to be honest about the ways the abuse has affected our ability to be ourselves, to feel pleasure, to make good choices. *I can't stand up for myself at work. I don't ever get erotic sensation in my, um, vagina. I feel like I don't deserve to get myself new clothes or to eat well. I can't stop having sex with married men.* The guiding principle in the group was that we'd done nothing wrong and nothing to warrant the traumatic circumstances that led us there. We were not fundamentally damaged. *I am not damaged.* They had us repeat this. I resented it, it felt like denial. *I am damaged*, I told them, that's why I was in the group. *I can also be damaging to others.* That's being alive for most people. They told us that looking at our pain squarely, processing it, expressing it, was precisely what the world did not want us to do. Refusing to live in shame gave us power. To be able to find pleasure again was necessary resistance. I mostly believed all that, and yet. At no point was I not overwhelmed with disgust. It made me jumpy and livid, listening to the voices inevitably crack, mine included. I could hear myself in them. I hated that I wanted to believe that enduring abuse was proof of something profound about my character—not, like, the second most common thing in the world next to shitting. *We can thank our pain for making us wise*, one of the group members said, *we have to come to some kind of peace.* There must be something beyond this, but what. There must be a letting go, but what in me dies if I do that. None of us wanted to be stuck like we were, inert, controlled by the symptoms of our history. Everyone was looking for the smartest way forward. Although it all felt preconditioned, there were only so many choices to help us move on. Own it, grieve it privately, bury it gracefully, celebrate survival, make art, find a god, or maybe decide to buck up, the victim narrative is pathetic. I'm not sure where I fell. Where I fall.

At the beginning with P.T., I really wanted-wanted him. I'd never felt that before with such intensity. I recognized I could go somewhere with him that I'd never gone with anyone else—too far. I had dated before, but not much. I dated men and women in college; nothing felt right. The closer I technically got to these people, the more time spent with them, the further away I felt. I couldn't explain the dark way I experienced the world, and I, perhaps naively, didn't think any of my potential lovers felt a similar existential burden. Then came P.T. That dark mouth. Those obsidian marbles for eyes. The energy he carried around like a ghost with shackles. I *recognized* him.

It's only recently I've begun to suspect that love and struggle are not necessarily one enterprise. Complete emotional absence isn't a difference in communication style, it's neglect. Violence is not a defensible by-product of lust or intensity, it's just violence. But I never feel relief when these realizations arise. I feel like a fool. They should be self-evident.

And what Screaming Bird Girl says about karma. That burns, too. My childhood, my relationship with P.T., it did feel like these things chose me. And haven't moved on. Maybe I've known on some level that we aren't through. If he's back, I guess it doesn't only feel unsafe, it feels like moving on is not possible, healing is not for me, and what I've feared all along is actually true—I got what I deserved. If he's here, then all my attempts to create boundaries are for naught. I am a magnet for this. He might actually be my fate. So yeah, I get her, obviously. There is still a deep part of me that believes what she thinks and even wants it to be true. But I also know there is no chance in hell she and Robbie will end well. Or, like my situation with P.T., it might never really end.

We change the subject after that. She asks me if I've been to Jitlada, the famous Thai place across the street. I have, I tell her. Really good green curry.

Finally, Courtney comes out with a bunch of broken-down boxes and lets us inside. I tell Courtney again about the trash at my door and ask again about cameras but she deflects. Once I'm back in my apartment, I put on some calming classical music and, impulsively, send a text.

Hey there, it's Clarice

Sorry for delay

Happen to be free for a drink next week?

15

It's unforgivable that Rich is who I ask to accompany me to Afterlife, under the guise of a date. Particularly because I have been gracelessly avoiding Bunny, who, under normal circumstances, would be my wingwoman for such shenanigans. But she would not be down for this. I want to see if the red-haired bartendress is finally back and just so happens to remember flirting with a certain customer she had about a month ago. I figure being on a date will make me seem less like a freak when I start probing her. Rich looks like a millennial Teletubby, one of those people who feels the burden of the office is his entire lot in life.

The Screaming Birds are fighting again when he texts me to let me know he's outside. I pass a crescendo of "You fucking cocksucking cunt," "Shut up!" and the sound, once again, of something hard hitting a wall. It doesn't feel like a great omen.

Nor does the fact that Rich has combed his hair like a greaser. He's wearing a vintage-style Led Zeppelin shirt under a pinstripe blazer. Rightfully, noticeably, he gives my Lakers hat and large purple zip-up a flummoxed once-over. It didn't even occur to me to change. I've been dressing like a stay-at-home dad for so long now. The first time I went on a date with P.T. I was wearing heeled sandals and a vintage wrap dress patterned with tiny peppermints, probably a thong.

"Didn't take me for a sports fan, did you?" I say, and he

laughs. He gently leans forward for a hug and I pretend not to notice. His car is the cleanest I've ever been in, smells stiffly of Altoids and Febreze. A box of Kleenex sits, poised, on the back seat.

Accompanied by the ominous whiz of his hybrid sedan, Rich launches into what sounds like a pre-prepared speech about how much he loves live music, despite being a litigator for corporate architects. Apparently he used to have a band in college with a few "science dudes" called Soiled. I don't comment on the name. He was the bass player and, from time to time, he says, wore eye makeup.

"You paved the way for these kids, Rich," I say, putting on my sunglasses and rearranging my cap as we pull into the lot behind Afterlife. Rich launches himself out of the car upon parking and comes around to my side. I pop open the door after a few moments of his fumbling with the embedded handle on the other side, trying, but failing, to do it for me.

Inside, I dart immediately toward the bar. I get a bitters and soda; he has a glass of sauvignon blanc after being told by a young bartender in low-slung jean shorts that they "don't fuck with martinis." The glass of wine is no taller than an iPhone. I feel sad as I watch him take a sip.

"So, how do you know Nicole and Tiff?" he asks, trying to catch my eye as it wanders all about the bar, looking for Amanda.

"Oh, well, we're like family now, but Bunny is the original connection. She and I were roommates in college. She's my best friend."

"She was kind of a wild child from what I gathered."

"We both were. We've calmed considerably. I barely even drink anymore," I say, lifting my beverage.

He blushes, discernibly. He must be realizing that mutual drunkenness is usually his path to sex. We take a stand at a café table; I position myself to see the bar and discreetly stand on tippy-toes in my sneakers. Onstage, a bunch of guys wearing large hooded capes go up and begin to chant.

"I bet you wish you were on a date with one of those cool guys up there, don't you," he jokes, obviously clocking that my mind is elsewhere. I shift back to my heels. A flulike ache crawls up my legs.

"Just nervous, Rich, that's all."

"Well, you need not be," he says, placing his damp palm on my hand, which is gripping the table's edge. As I slide out from under his non-clasp, I see her. Amanda. The Bartendress. I have a proper shiver as I watch her talk to the other bartender. She opens the register and takes, from below the cash tray, an envelope I assume contains her tips. Her coworker hands her a box of cigarettes. Rich playfully reaches to poke me on the arm to get my attention back, but I make the moment extremely physically awkward by lifting my drink at the same time. His finger lands on my side rib, somewhat painfully. We say nothing about it.

"Rich, do you smoke?" I say suddenly as I see Amanda heading toward the side door to the smoking patio. I delight in remembering there is no exit back there.

"Oh, god no. People still smoke?" he says, dismissive.

"I'm gonna pop outside." I give him a "one minute" gesture, then shoot to the courtyard. I spot her, sitting on the corner of a picnic table, cigarette lit, looking at her phone. I side-shuffle through a group of youths. Their bodies send off a general sex-seeking-missile heat that registers to my body like felt pressure. Bits of conversation rise from the crowd as I pass. "Not no, bitch." "Tallulah's poly now?" "They should make Impossible Tilapia."

When I get to Amanda's table, I give a flimsy wave and ask to join her there. She barely acknowledges me. A beat passes and I lean toward her.

"I can assure you I'm not drunk . . . ," I say, even though I feel truly dizzy with nerves and mentally a few seconds ahead of real time. She puts up her hand in a stop gesture. She has acrylic nails, I notice, but a tip is broken off on the pointer finger. She reaches into her pocket and brings out the package of clove cigarettes her coworker gave her, something I haven't had since middle school. I take one, thanking her, letting her light it, and, with effort, make a yum sound. It tastes like a Yankee Candle. Bartendress Amanda continues to stare at her phone. I awkwardly shuffle myself on the bench and remark on the beautiful night. She looks up at me and says, "I know, right?" then back down at her phone.

"Can I ask you something?" I say, after a minute.

"Uh," she says, "sure." I take a deep breath as she raises her gaze. She looks more tired than I expected. She's young but has the bottomless eyes of a heavy drinker—equal parts happy and sad. It makes me think, very briefly, that I should ask her my strange questions in the context of the truth.

"So, I was here like, two weeks ago, and I saw you talking to this guy," I begin shakily, immediately deciding against the truth idea.

"Yeah?"

"Yeah."

She shoots some air out of her nose. "I talk to a lot of guys, hon."

"Well, you were talking for a while, it seemed. He had like dark gold curlyish hair? And he was sitting at the bar, wearing a bomber jacket. And he was pouring wax on his hand from one of the bar candles? Then on your hand."

She looks confused and uncomfortable.

"Oh, actually . . ." She clears her throat and puts out her half-finished clove on the corner of the table, which is marked with ashy circles from countless similar gestures. "Yes, I know who you're talking about."

"You do!" I say. I'm almost squealing, unable to control my volume.

"He's your boyfriend?" She sets the question down like a weight.

"No, that's not why I'm asking!"

"Good, because we fucked," she says, her body relaxing.

"Right," I say, feeling suddenly warm and high. If it is him, I have to warn her, right? That's the thing to do? "I was just wondering if you can remind me of his name. I think we might have gone to this study abroad program together and I wanted to see if . . ." I clear my throat, to keep from choking on my own clove-flavored spit. She squints, then breaks into a little smile.

"You know, it's so funny you're asking his name," she says.

"Why is that?" I suddenly imagine he did see me, maybe before I saw him. That he pointed me out, told her that I was insane, had framed him and tried to ruin his life. That didn't occur to me. Maybe he had followed me to the bar in the first place.

"I'm trying to *remember* his fucking name."

"Oh?"

"Yeah. We had insane, amazing sex. Twice. And we've been sexting since then. He left town for a minute, went up north, and then he was busy when he came back. He's finally supposed to come over again tomorrow night."

"Oh, no kidding." Holy shit.

"But like, I cannot for the fucking life of me remember his name. I couldn't the next morning. Not a chance in hell I can ask at this point. And to be honest, I'm actually starting to like him."

"Well, you could ask how he spells it."

"But what if it's like 'Pete'?"

"Is it Pete?" My pulse quickened. Pete. So close to P.T.

Practically is P.T. How could she have guessed that name? This no-man's-land of an answer is a punishment. The universe is kicking me in the crotch.

"That's what I mean, I don't know! I was so coked out, we were both drunk," she goes on. "And like, he fully knows my name, he keeps leaving these sexy voice notes."

"Can I hear one?" I ask, too fast.

"Um, no . . ." She looks confused.

"I'm joking, obviously."

"Yeah. Why didn't you come up to him and say hi?" she asks. I notice my clove is about an inch and a half of ash at this point, which I flick and watch gently snow to the ground.

"I didn't want to interrupt flirting, especially because, you know, I wasn't totally sure if it was him. But then I did want to find a way to reach out, if he was in town, because I heard through the grapevine that this guy's, maybe the guy you were talking to . . . his twin brother . . . actually was lost, or like, died, I mean, in a boating thing," I say, feeling a sense of pride and surprise at how easily the story is flowing. "A boating accident. So, I didn't want to bring that up right then. If it was him. Especially if I didn't remember his name. And I'm no longer in touch with the person who, like, told me about the accident, so I couldn't—"

"Oh my god, so sad!" she exclaims, and then her expression shifts, her mouth opens a little. "Fuck—there's no way he could have told me that, right? I would remember that, right?"

"I'm sure he didn't . . ."

"Amanda."

"Amanda," I say. "I'm Jude."

"I really, deeply wish I had an answer for you, Jude." She laughs again and runs her hand through her plentiful hair. "And it's just more proof that I need to quit this job before I die a pitiful, alcoholic death."

"We've all been there," I say, biting my tongue.

"Have you checked Insta?"

"I'm not on Insta," I lie, immediately fearing that she'll show my profile to P.T. I then kick myself because it rules out showing her his feed, not that any of the images of him are particularly clear as it is. I remember I took a screenshot of the tagged picture of P.T. in Griffith Park—I start scrolling through my photos.

"Oh god, no socials, epic. Well, this guy is on there," she says. "But he wouldn't give me his handle when I asked the night we met, and I haven't asked again. He said the less we know about each other's past the better. Which is hot but maybe scary?"

"Yeah, there's something maybe a little off about that, but hey—I do actually have this old picture of my friend that I, uh, found when I was trying to figure this out . . . can I show you?" I say, shoving my phone in her sight line, zoomed in on P.T. sitting on the grass. "Is this the guy you slept with?"

She cranes her neck back, widens her eyes. "Um, okay, wow . . . well, yeah, it looks like his hair, but he's looking down? I can't see his face, girl."

"But would you say the aura of the person you know is similar to the aura in this photo?"

"What?" she asks, dubious. "Are you sure you guys didn't fuck?"

"No, no, no, I'm joking about the aura. That was a bit."

"Right . . . do you want me to just ask him if he knows you?"

My eyes go wide. I reach over, laboriously, awkwardly, to smash my clove butt as she did. "Um, sure, no harm in asking if he knows Jude . . . Doggins."

She looks down at her phone as it buzzes, then raises her eyebrows.

"Speak of the fucking devil, Jude Doggins."

"It's him?" Like he heard me through the ether.

"Yeah, he just texted," she says, typing back to him. "I have him saved under O Guy, because he—"

"I get it!" My voice betrays me again and cracks at the exact wrong moment. I feel P.T. on the other side of her phone, as though he somehow knows I'm here standing next to this pretty woman who thinks she's talking to a regular schmo. The library of his dick pics I deleted from my phone rolls through my brain; so does the plethora of nudes he had of me. *Your nudes bring to mind both Egon Schiele and Richard Kern*, he told me once as I quietly tensed a fist in victory. I had pined for any occasion of sexual flattery from him. The sweet, satisfying flavors he assigned to the taste of my crotch, the exceptionally solid boners he told me I inspired, how my ass felt so soft it was as though I'd never once sat down.

"Well . . ." She speaks aloud as she types. "I can't wait to sit on your face." She looks up at me. "Is that a grossly on-the-nose thing to write?"

"Not for a liberated woman." She hasn't clocked my horrified expression. She's thinking about how many orgasms P.T. has given her. How is it possible he is so adept at the female orgasm? A Faustian bargain? Am I sure he truly made me come, or does my self-delusion run deeper than I thought was possible?

"Does this guy . . . does he have a hand tattoo?" I think to ask as I push away an image of the coyote tattoo sliding into my thighs.

"Yeah, he has a hand tattoo. A bunch of tattoos, but I don't know what all of them are. Anyway!" Her phone drops as she haphazardly throws up her hands in a gesture of surrender. I pick it up and give it back to her, noticing that her screen is cracked down the middle both vertically and horizontally, almost a perfect Christ's cross. As is mine. This seems cosmic. "So, gotta roll. Just came for my tips. I'm fucking beat. Good meeting you."

When I run back inside the minute after she does, the ice in my drink has mostly melted and Rich looks forlorn.

"I thought you left," he says faintly.

"There's no exit back there," I say, putting my hand on his shoulder. "Rich, listen, I need to ask you an unusual favor."

"Okay . . ."

"It's an unusual favor that is also creepy."

"Oh, boy." He laughs a little, chucks back the last half-inch of his miniature wine drink. His cheeks and nose are booze-flushed, as though his blushing earlier stayed put.

"Do you see that beautiful red-haired woman behind the bar there?" I point at Amanda the Bartendress, who is throwing about her arms in conversation with her coworker. Rich tenses his jaw but looks over at Amanda, then back at me. Behind us, more droning vocals start.

"She is about to leave here. And we need to leave right now, get in your car, and follow her back to her house."

"Is she having a party?"

I stop for a second, consider telling a lie—perhaps we could get there and I could feign social anxiety. But I owe Rich some truth.

"No, she's not."

"Are you buying drugs?"

"Also no."

"Do you want us to have a . . ."

I snort. "Sorry. No. It's not you, or her for that matter, it's me."

He shrugs and gets up. I assume he's going to tell me I'm a bad person and leave me without a ride. Instead he points his thumb toward the door.

"Okay. Let's go then. We'll want to be in the car already when she comes out."

I follow behind him as he leads the way outside, a little bounce in my step, like a child en route to the toy store.

"Is there a staff lot?" he asks after we get into his car.

"No, I don't think so," I say. I'm impressed. "Rich, is there a reason this isn't strange to you?"

"This will seem random, and perhaps to your good fortune, but I used to be a PI. Out of the game for good, but it's how I put myself through law school."

"You're fucking with me."

"I'm not. It's a dirty business, but a part of me lives for the adventure. My guess is Code Red over there, coming out now, is either an ex of yours, someone an ex of yours is sleeping with, or someone you suspect of stealing something from you."

"Wow," I say. "Code Red. I like that."

"I worked mostly on adultery cases when I was out there," he said. "I played a pivotal role in many divorces."

"That's great, Rich," I say. I notice he adjusts his rearview to watch her get into her car. He takes his car out of park and slowly starts to reverse, saying, "Go time," in a voice just above a whisper. A swell of excitement blossoms in my chest. We lag a bit behind her with an eerie and smooth slowness. Elton John's "Candle in the Wind" plays as we go. It seems to give me the spiritual strength to tell him what's going on with P.T. The abbreviated version, anyway.

"You've checked the net, I assume. You and he have no mutual contacts?"

"We don't. I haven't heard anything about him since the restraining order went through."

We follow Code Red all the way to a small Craftsman in Silver Lake. If I had to guess I'd say we're talking 2.5 mil of real estate, so she's either bartending for fun or has roommates. He parks across the street and we watch her go inside.

"So, she told you he's coming tomorrow night?"

"That's right," I say.

"It will probably be late, I'd stake just after eight to be safe. You want the sun down. Don't sit in the back seat, if you were thinking about it. It frightens people. Plus, if you need to tail one of them, you want to be ready to go. Bring a book, talk on the phone. Like you're waiting. Wear a hat. Do you have a wig?"

"Uh . . ."

"That's fine. There's plenty of cars parked on this street so I can't imagine she'll clock you, but there's also enough space that I'm not concerned about parking. And you might want to borrow Bunny's car, just to be extra cautious."

"She's not really in support of these endeavors. You don't think I could borrow yo—"

"No."

"Fair."

"I'll tell you what, this is technically illegal but as civilians we can bend the rules. I'll go out in a minute and evaluate the premises. Just to see where you can stake for a sight line indoors if you can't ID him as he enters."

"And what happens if I figure out it's him?"

"You just figure it out. My expertise stops there."

He gets out and walks to the back of the house. I lean my forehead to the cool of the passenger window to watch him and it calms me, might be the nicest sensation I've felt all day.

My phone buzzes then. It alarms me so much when I see who is calling that I let out a little yell. Dad. For the second time in a month, the second time in years. I look at the screen, hold it while it buzzes and I miss the call, still staring at the screen a good minute later when VOICEMAIL pops up. I consider deleting it without listening, my thumb hovering. I already feel the tinny pressure of the migraine that descends each time I hear his voice. In combination with my current situation, it might cause a seizure. I do nothing for a few long minutes.

Rich gets into the car, his eyes bright and wide.

"Huge windows, yard sloping upward in the back, and plenty of trees," he says with speed. "Best view of the upstairs would be getting some lift from the yard over, which, luckily for you, is vacant. So who's to say you're not checking out real estate. Prime escape route, too. Look at that magnolia tree right there, very sturdy branches toward the bottom."

I smile at him, feeling foggy with overwhelm. "Awesome."

"What's wrong? You want to back out from the mission?" He exhales, deflated. I smell garlic.

"Nothing," I say.

"You don't seem excited any longer, Clarice," says Rich. The sound of pity in his voice makes me want to insult him, but I hold back. He's being kind to me. Too kind.

"My dad called when you were in there."

"Oh, god, is he okay?"

"I didn't pick up. We're estranged."

Rich looks uneasy, and who can blame him. He happens to be the person I've chosen to share the entirety of this craziness with, and I can safely say both of us are not sure why. I need at least one person to know everything that's going on, and unfortunately it can't be anyone I know and love. He awkwardly reaches over and puts a hand on my shoulder, his mouth puckered. I wonder if he's considering my mental stability. When this is all over, I should probably send him a gift basket.

"I am just trying to decide whether or not to delete the voicemail."

"Sure," Rich says, reaching over me to open the glove box and take out a bag of Jolly Ranchers. He offers me one, which I take. He takes two, then puts them on the dash.

"I don't think he's all there anymore. He's mostly paralyzed. I think he has wet brain."

"Oh, that is . . . a very uncomfortable life."

"Too true. He drinks, smokes, and watches TV. Which are the only things he's enjoyed for the last twenty years, anyway."

"How could he smoke?" Rich asks, confused.

"My imagination has decided that his girlfriend holds cigarettes up to his mouth," I say, and I watch that image land in Rich's head like it hurts him.

"Listen," Rich lets out after a moment, "if you don't want to erase it, and you don't want to hear it, why don't you read the transcription."

"Right. That is something I could do." I look down at my phone, press the voicemail. Of course, it says UNABLE TO TRANSCRIBE. I lean over and show Rich.

"I mean, I have no skin in the game. I can listen to it," Rich says. "Again, I had to examine a lot of personal correspondence in my day. It doesn't faze me."

"Rich, you've done enough. Honestly. This is a truly bizarre turn of events for what was supposed to have been a date."

"What else would I be doing tonight?"

"I don't know."

"Here, why don't you play it and we can both listen?"

I look over at him, softening. He nods once. My hands are still shaking a little. I hate being a human. I hate the part of me that still reacts to my dad's voice. Hearing it makes me want to talk to him. It makes me confused. I want to gain the power to turn back time, give him the opportunity to do life ever so slightly better. I dread his death daily, I'm watching the clock like it will be the only thing to ever liberate me, I hate him, I want him, I miss him, I have no idea who he is or what he wants from me.

I press play. I hear the sustained clearing of a throat, some shuffling. Then about seven to ten seconds of static, like someone is rubbing fabric against the mic, and then what sounds, unfortunately, like a muffled fart.

"Was that . . . ?" Rich asks.

"I think so," I say.

"Not purposefully, of course?"

"Who knows."

I look ahead into the streetlights reflecting off cars. Not sure what I wanted to happen, what I wanted to hear. One unintentional voicemail fart and now I'm thinking about this picture I have in a keepsake box of him as a little kid, standing on his front porch. He's holding his hands behind his back, his ears stuck out like arrows, wearing a huge, horse-toothed, crescent-moon smile.

I anxiously bite at a hangnail and look out the window of Rich's car, noticing, just then, that there is a new car in Code Red's driveway.

"Oh, fuck!" I yell. Rich and I both jump a little.

"What?"

"Another car! We missed him!" Warp speed, I recline my passenger seat. "Do you think he saw me?"

"Absolutely not," Rich says, opening the center console, taking out a pair of Solar Shield sunglasses and handing them to me. "And we don't know if it's him. I thought you said he was coming tomorrow."

"He probably couldn't wait," I groan. "He probably couldn't wait until tomorrow, because he's like that. Lustful!"

"Listen, that could be a roommate, a friend. And if it is P.T., he has to leave sometime." He pops out of the car before I can stop him, walks casually over, leans his body toward the window of the parked car to look.

"It's not him," he says, getting back in, and with him, this time, a pleasant whiff of jacaranda. "In the passenger seat there's a half-eaten MacroBar and a copy of *Where the Crawdads Sing*. That sticker in the corner of the back window is a La Cañada high school teacher's parking pass."

"I appreciate you, Rich," I say, watching him take his cap off, noticing a small V of sweat has gathered beneath the collar of his vintage-style tee. “I really do.” Rich tells me it’s no problem, he’s happy to help, and that it’s probably time for him to head home.

When Rich drops me off ten minutes later, there’s an ambulance and two police cars outside of my house. Not great. I get the thought that P.T. tried to break in and was attacked by one of the building kooks while I was with Rich—but then it dawns on me. Screaming Bird Girl. The threats were there, and we all heard them. He said countless times he was going to kill her. Because love means going to the farthest possible point, she told me as much herself, just days ago. Two men bring a stretcher inside, and people are gathered in the street. I see Courtney on the opposite sidewalk, talking to a cop. I sidle up next to her.

“She finally fucking did it,” she says, not turning her head, when the cop goes back to his car and she notices me standing there.

“Huh?”

“The woman on the first floor? The couple that fights? She stabbed him. I would have done it, too, honestly.”

“You’re fucking kidding.”

“I’m not.”

“I really thought it was going to be the other way around,” I say. I’m shocked. I wonder if Bird Girl knew this was about to happen, deep down, as we were having that conversation.

“We all did, Clarice. I mean, people complained about them constantly. He’s not dead or anything, either, just like, so bloody and freaked. It’s not a cute scene. I got in there and he’s got these two stabs right through his jeans on his thigh, and like, pretty deep, you know, and he’s crying, screaming that she’s gone and he’s going to die.”

"Holy hell, I'm sorry, Courtney."

"We're also not sure where she went," Courtney says. "I guess she filled a backpack and bolted."

"So, she's on the lam? Just gone?" I ask. Courtney shrugs. She looks worn out. It's a harsh truth that moments like these are when you notice someone's roots are showing, their skin lacks luster.

"It's never easy to witness this stuff. No matter how many times," she says, taking a pack of chewing gum from her pocket, offering me a piece. She pops one from the sheet into my waiting palm.

"A stabbing has happened here before?"

"Oh, loads. This management company has a few locations. One time a teen mom stuck a fork in a toddler's forearm."

"That image is now seared in my brain."

"Tell me about it," she says. "But this time, it's the *stabber* who I really hope is okay."

"Yeah, same," I say, wondering what it was that finally made Screaming Bird Girl crack. It's macabre, but I'm proud of her. "Can I go inside or is it like a crime scene?"

"No, you can go." She nods. We stand there for a second with our arms crossed, watching the paramedics heave Screaming Bird Guy awkwardly down the steps on a rolling stretcher. Every bump on the stair, a loud moan. His eyes are closed, his face distorted in agony and self-pity. He's clutching the wounds on his thighs. She left his stomach intact, his heart, and it makes me think that perhaps injury is worse, in some ways, than death. Men like that can't take much discomfort at all, and if she hit a nerve or sliced a muscle or something, this will bother him for the rest of his life. My guess is he was coming at her, of course, and it was self-defense. But it might have just been a moment of quiet. Knife in the hand, he's sitting there eating yogurt, and BAM! She does it. I hope she is far off somewhere, feeling light as a butterfly, already dyeing her hair.

16

While I waited for the second court date, time melted together. I was watching TV in the dead of winter, looked up, and it was spring. Very occasionally I'd go out for a beer with Maxine. Nicole was in town on business for a few days in March and I took MDMA and went dancing at a gay bar with her, something Tiff hated to do. But that was it. P.T. never contacted me during this time, and there was a shy sense of hope in that.

It was maybe a week before my scheduled court date in late April. I was with Maxine outside our apartment, each of us leaning against the building with a square piece of pizza we'd gotten from around the block. The air was cold but the sun was making me overheat in my coat.

"This is how I'm thinking about it, Maxine. He hasn't contacted me. When I saw him in January, it honestly made me want to walk into the sea with rocks in my pockets. I don't want to go through that again. And he hasn't contacted me. So I'm just going to not show up, and effectively let it drop."

"It's your choice," she said, "but I think you should go."

I took a bite and chewed sloppily. "I'll take that into consideration." I watched her start to say something, then stop herself, which was unusual. It seemed she was being as patient with me as she could muster, and I appreciated that.

Of course, Maxine was right. The morning came and I watched the clock, watched the hour pass by when I should have been in court. Maxine was out of town for a couple of days for a design conference—which she offered to skip, until I insisted she not—so it was just me, no one pushing me last-minute to go in. I made some coffee and toast, cut a cantaloupe, sat and stared at a wall. Exactly an hour after I was meant to be in court, my phone dinged with an email from a name I didn't recognize. Mike Watertower.

Clarice,

I missed seeing you in court this afternoon. As your foolish order is no longer in place I would like to set a time for us to meet together privately. I am willing to put this horror behind us and have only good energy going forward.

Believe it or not, I do not hold any resentment against you about all of this. But I am saddened you didn't show up. I wanted to see you in person. I would like to talk to you in private. Just the two of us. I still have an apology that I want to give to you. Can you find the compassion to take a small amount of time to listen to a brokenhearted man?

I know this will not end, and will not go away, until you are able to do that for me.

Astonished, I read it again. All that registered was the dull absence of feeling. I tried to force tears by scrunching up my face and coughing, to have some kind of release, but I was wound too tight.

I walked back down to the court, alone this time. In a daze through security, then waiting in the pew outside the courtroom, waiting for a judge. Feeling gravity pull at my skin. Near me sat this young guy, wavy hair, down puffer, maybe nineteen. "I know you probably think I brought this on somehow," he said to an older woman who looked deeply annoyed. Presumably his mother. "But she didn't seem crazy or scary. She's rich, she's cultured. She gets good grades!"

When I went in, it was a different judge. He had me explain the whole timeline again, then explain why I didn't show up, then explain why I was coming back to get another order. I told him about P.T. asking to meet me in private, telling me he loved and missed me.

"You know I saw him a few hours ago? He said you're making all this up."

"Well, I'm not," I said. "I thought he got the message."

"Who gets the message?" he asked. But then he granted it because he'd told P.T. to leave me alone that morning, and that next time the judge wouldn't be so nice. He told me they would probably not serve the order until Monday. He said next time I came back to court, since I wanted a longer-term protective order, we would be going to trial. I wasn't sure what that meant, but I didn't want to ask. He gave me the date. Then he shooed me out the door with a little wave, like he was guiding away a bug.

When I got outside, I checked my phone. I had already received another long email from P.T. He was technically and legally able to contact me at that moment—until they served him again—and he was back in a big way.

The subject line was "FYI: LAWSUIT COMING YOUR WAY!"

At first I was devastated you didn't show up at court, on further thought, I'm filled with rage. Thus, I've decided to sue you for 30,000 dollars. First of all, for wasting my damn time. Also for slander, and egregious misuse of the court process, etc. For multiple weeks of lost work and indescribable emotional damages. I have already sued you in small claims court for $5,000—you should be receiving that paperwork any day now. Remember that I know your address? Don't think this means I'm no longer in love with you. I am. And I stand proudly by my desire to speak with you in person so we can work things out. If you agree to do *that I am very likely to drop these charges I will be placing/have placed against you.*

It went on. He admitted he had narcissistic traits and could be unfeeling toward others at times but ultimately he was not emotionally built to be dealing with the court system. He was too fragile. All he did was cry, he said. Have some pity, he said. In the next two days, he sent me thirteen emails from a new email address. In one of them he told me he could see I was reading them.

The next day, when Maxine was back, she had a few friends and family members over for dinner and I joined. I got pretty drunk, everyone did, but at one point I started oversharing about my life and began to cry. Maxine whispered something to her cousin, whose name I may never know, and he asked me later to come outside for a breather with him as he had a cigarette.

The moment we got outdoors the cousin launched into a story about a friend of his having an affair with their college professor. I think he was trying to communicate that everyone makes mistakes? I was so woozy that I couldn't follow but I kept nodding—even when I saw P.T. over the cousin's shoulder, coming down the sidewalk with a big trash bag. What I assume would have been a few of my things, or maybe a pillow and a handgun. I froze. I watched P.T. stop and look around. He must have clocked Maxine's cousin, who had turned more onto the sidewalk and into his line of sight. I knew he wouldn't approach me if I was with a man. For whatever reason, I didn't tell Maxine about that when I went upstairs. I didn't tell anyone.

Early the next morning, another email.

Clarice,

Is that tall man your new boyfriend?

A song was attached that he wrote entitled “Rips, Tears/Tears.” I couldn’t bring myself to listen. I just sent it all along to Bunny, who called me immediately to express her concern, and Maxine, who emailed me right back.

What boyfriend? He is completely & unwaveringly INSANE.

Monday morning you need to address this attempt at threats & bullshit with a lawyer. I might have a contact.

x

Maxine

I met my lawyer, Jason Beranji, at a Starbucks, months before we were supposed to go to trial. He shared his office with his dad—a firm called Beranji Squared—and because it was a tight fit, he took meetings at this particular West Fifty-Seventh location. Everyone starts somewhere. He was willing to take the case for $750 a day, apparently a steal. He had an okay rating on ratelawyers.com, too, 7.6. Which is great, because people hate lawyers. I told him I’d be in a green coat. He told me he’d be in Dockers and a windbreaker.

He was younger than I expected. I was thinking midforties despite the office share. He was just cresting thirty. Straightforward, subtly sloppy, blood of the tristate area coursing through him. Relatively good-looking with a paunch and sparsely gelled hair. Could have used a lint roller on his pants. When I’d called him on the phone the other day, I was expecting to feel uncomfortably vulnerable about my situation—having to tell a stranger about the exceptionally poor choices I’d made leading up to all this. But after I told him the basics, he spent a long few minutes selling himself to me. This would be a symbiotic pairing, it seemed.

“Clarice?” He said it like “Clawreese,” which was how the

guy at the deli on Twenty-Third said my name when I was a kid, before the move and the divorce, when the world felt like my own huge, dirty, walkable playground. It gave me a cozy feeling. "Jason Beranji. You want something more to drink? Snack on?"

I shook my head and wondered who would really be buying if I said yes. He sat down and ordered something on his Starbucks app. I had brought in my own cortado from a nicer place, and judging by his breath, he'd already had a few himself.

"Do anything fun this weekend?" I asked him as he slid around in his canvas briefcase for our contract. He bobbed his head to the pop standard playing overhead.

"I proposed to my girlfriend."

"And?" I said, attempting to rustle up some excitement for him.

"She's now my fiancée."

"A hearty congratulations!" I lifted my coffee in cheers, spilling a little on my hand, quickly licking it up. "How'd you do it?"

"I trailed rose petals in the hall, had Jon Batiste on. Champagne."

"Can't go wrong with tradition!" He looked proud, and I couldn't judge him for that. "Were you nervous?"

"I mean, she's been hinting at me for a year now, pointing out rings, the whole bit. But still. You never know."

"You never do." I watched in real time as he registered how he was talking about his romantic joy to a person he was helping to legally restrain an ex-lover. His face betrayed this so clearly I almost laughed. Me, victim and mayhem magnet; him, normal on a cellular level, a UAlbany lawyer who undoubtedly drove a midrange luxury vehicle. He placed his contract, obviously formatted on MS Word, in front of me and handed me a ballpoint. I signed without reading.

"So, that's it for now?"

"That's it for now. Come in a couple days before the trial and we can prepare."

"How should I prepare for preparing?"

"I mean, there's not much. You know, we've got the email printouts, the texts, you've got the timeline of his weird behavior after the breakup. We've talked all that through. We'll just talk it through again."

"Right."

"You still have those gifts he gave you, right?"

"Yeah, yeah."

"Great. I'll provide the other stuff, you make sure you bring the gifts and that *Family Life* magazine subscription or whatever it was he sent you. Then it's up to the gods of justice." He spotted his coffee, grabbed it, and pursed his lips to blow at the tiny hole on the lid.

"Okay. Sounds like a plan, I guess."

His expression changed from casual to solemn. "That said, I mean, I'll reiterate this. As your lawyer. As I told you before. He didn't threaten murder, he didn't break into your house, we've got no bruise pictures, no physical abuse. That can make this kind of thing a tough case. I've seen judges tell people to talk it out among themselves in situations where there's no violence or written or recorded threats. You know, they're like, 'What's the problem? Love stinks.' That kind of thing. So we gotta hope for, you know . . ." He made a vague back-and-forth gesture with his hands I couldn't interpret.

". . . What are we hoping for?" I asked, after a pause, just as a pockmarked employee leaned over the counter, yelling, "Alan! Cold foam!"

"Honestly, a female judge is our hope," he said to me finally as he cracked his neck with a quick jerk, his voice notably lowered. "Not to paint anybody with a broad brush, but generally the New York women of the court, sort of, well, unless they're kind of traditional, you know, they . . ."

"Understand nuance? Or nuances of violation, I guess?"

"Nuances of violation, yeah, that's good," he said, then took out his phone and began, I believe, typing that phrase into his notes app. He jerked his head back up, looking at me intensely. I noticed a little crud in the corner of his left eye. "Did I mention you aren't really going to talk much?"

"No."

"Well, you aren't. But if you do speak out of turn, for example, it's not like the judge can unhear whatever it is you say. You see what I'm getting at?"

"Um, I don't know. What's an example of that?" I asked. "Of a thing I can't say but it wouldn't hurt if I said it?"

"Like, something that happened before you broke up, for example. You know, like maybe he did something insane."

"We were both kind of insane."

"Yeah, don't say that."

"Got it."

"That said . . ." Jason shrugged. "I mean, if he did anything really sketchy, if you were to drop that in somehow . . ." Then he stopped himself, put a finger to his chin. "On the other hand, it's hard to strike a balance because you don't want to make it seem like you're getting some kind of revenge . . ."

I struggled to accept that the whole legal process was truly this much of a dog-and-pony show, up to what seemed like the whims and wind patterns of a few black-robe-wearing overachievers.

"Another tip, you don't necessarily want to come into court looking happy and well rested, but definitely well-kept, normal. And no new lovers."

I laughed a little and decided not to ask him to elaborate, nor did I tell him that it wouldn't be a problem, since I wasn't happy or looking for love. Even though I sometimes slept for what seemed like days at a time, I was never well rested. *I was born exhausted, Jason.* I would probably forever remain that way.

"I'll keep that in mind, Jason," I said. "Oh, also, he sued me in small claims court for five grand? That's bad, right? I don't know if he's doing it as a fake-out threat. In one of the emails he sent, he said he would drop it. Do you think I should go?"

"*Oh, yeah.* If you don't show up and he does? Likely you're gonna owe him that five K."

"Are you kidding?"

"I wish I was. Tell me the date and I'll block it off."

We said our goodbyes and I watched him walk uptown against the spring wind, his hair standing up as he went. He had chosen the right coat, that windbreaker. I hoped that boded well.

17

I'm at a very LA upscale pharmacy when Damian calls around 9 a.m. I barely slept and I'm tweaked from the strange night with Rich—not to mention the Screaming Birds crime—so I decide to take care of that with some new concealer and multivitamins. The dark circles are beginning to look like terminal illness. I tried to ignore his first two calls, but a woman next to me looking at probiotic face cream asked if I was "going to get that" when it rang the third time.

"Dude, what?" I say, one undereye heavily painted with an organic concealer tester—shade "Milky Natural"—the other not.

"Dad's been calling me, Clarice, almost daily." Damian lets out a dramatic sigh right into the mouthpiece of his phone. "He really wants to get ahold of you."

"Right, yeah, he called me."

"I'm worried about him," he says.

"More worried than the years he spent . . . not calling? Tell him I'll call him when I get the back payments for child support."

"He's dying."

"He made the bed he doesn't leave," I quip, feeling immediately guilty about the joke. On a good day, when I extend myself, I like to consider there is something almost Zen or anticapitalist in my father's lifelong refusal to work or to have any real attachments to anything other than alcohol and drugs.

Ironically, or poetically, his paralysis ensures that way of life will stay for him until the end.

"I know he's not a great man, Clarice. But I'm going to share something with you. When my boss's mother died, she chose not to say goodbye because her mother was horrible, and she regrets it. She feels no freedom in her passing."

"Uh, with love, I think I'll feel the freedom," I say, instantly doubting myself. I take a finger and try to transfer some of the concealer to the other eye while I walk toward the self-checkout.

"Clarice."

"And by your boss, do you mean the woman you call Sergeant Shitbreath?"

"Not to her face—anyway, no one uses that nickname anymore. She got her gums grafted and it seems to have fixed the issue. All beside the point."

"If you must know, Damian, Dad left me a message last night that said nothing, but I'm pretty sure I heard him fart."

"Well, he doesn't have control of his—"

"Can we please go back to only updating me about Dad when I ask?"

He stays silent on the line for a long time. So long, in fact, that I'm able to buy the concealer and start eating the chocolate-covered cashews I added at the last minute. Silence is what he does to refrain from criticizing me, which is what he used to do. I consider it growth.

In his meaner moments, Damian has said that I think "the trauma" is the most interesting thing about me, and that it controls me and ruins any sense of what I can accomplish. He's probably right, but, whatever. He says our life got pretty dark but in the grand scheme it wasn't that bad—we could have been living in a tent or been placed into the foster system. *My apologies but—everyone's a survivor now, Clarice*, he said once, half joking. *The online generation robbed us of any romance or dignity that might come along with that.* I mean, amen? I don't know. As far back as I can remember he's told me he doesn't really feel affected by our childhood, which makes me laugh. A gay man raised by insane failed artists chose to join a branch of the military and bought stocks with his savings starting at nineteen—he's the blueprint for rebellion through order.

Either way, Damian doesn't know the extent of my relationship with Dad. I don't know the extent of his, either, I suppose. We don't talk about specifics much. I think it feels too claustrophobic. Talking to Roz or Bunny about my past feels like I'm telling a story. Reminiscing with Damian feels like we're ripping off our skins and standing in the cold. Together we witnessed the hitting, the punched holes in the wall and kicked-in doors, the name-calling, the drunken psychosis. He bullied Damian when he was drunk. Or hungover. I remember Dad once told him to suck his cock when he was in elementary school. Dad didn't know how to deal with another masculine presence, especially since Damian was naturally tall and strong and very good at sports. Dad openly liked me more when we were little. He favored me.

When my boobs were suggesting themselves—they came early, yes, but I was generally still shapeless, a fingerling potato—I sensed a marked difference in how my dad acted toward me. Or maybe I just started to notice. How he interacted with my body, things he said to me. If we were alone he often kissed me on the lips when saying goodbye, *like Europeans*, he said, holding my cheeks, but it felt too long. Shoulder squeeze, knee squeeze, hand on thigh. That breath on the ear. Thumb swipe over my shirt. He used to lightly tickle my back to help me fall asleep, then he started to add in every other part of my body. He'd take showers with me. Not touch me, but just get in, he said, to preserve water, *we're family*. He'd ask me these odd questions sometimes, his eyes half-mast, high. *Do you think about what men find attractive? Do you think you know what men like?* He'd show me pictures of what men liked. He'd point it out in movies I shouldn't have been watching. It confused me, it still does. It's not clear what a person calls that behavior from a father. Roz says confusion is actually something that preserves you, saves you. As a kid you're just trying to seek love and attention, and you can't control what comes at you, you have to make some kind of sense of it. I remember smelling his underarm once, lying next to him in my bed. *I like how you smell*, I told him. Tobacco, chocolate, skin, Old Spice. *You know it's important to like how your lovers smell, Clarice. It makes it easier to get pregnant.*

I can't think about it for too long, and generally I don't. But it comes up. I remember a while back I was at Nicole and Tiff's and one of their daughters—she's nine, Frances—was dancing around the backyard with just her bathing suit bottoms on, running through the sprinkler, getting into the pool, sticking her fingers down her pants and smelling them. When I first saw her out there I felt so uncomfortable I wanted to throw up. I was angry they were letting her be naked like that, around other people. The reaction felt strange to me; I love their kids, I think they're great parents, not that anyone asked. I talked to Roz about it. *Think about it*, she said, *a little girl expressing herself in her body*, *safely*. There was no danger of her being violated, shamed. Her expressions came freely, she was unperturbed. No one was making her aware of herself.

Roz asked me to imagine what the energy of sexuality might look like at its very first stages. I said I guessed like light, like a prism. I saw a fountain made of glistening bug wings. She told me to imagine allowing that force to come alive and into itself, through expression and curiosity. *What might that process look like? Feel like? How could it grow in a healthy way?*

It's a vague instruction, of course, but I couldn't figure out anything to say. It was all ultimately disgusting and uncontrollable, no? By the time I was as old as Frances, I had already been marked by someone. A little plant, stepped on but still alive. When puberty really hit I became walled off and indelicate to repel unwanted attention. The idea that my sexuality could ever belong entirely to myself, that it had the potential to be filled with curiosity and excitement instead of bewilderment, didn't feel possible to me. Sex means dissociation. Sex means control or chaos, not much in between.

By the time I started having sex as a teenager—after my senior year, with my boyfriend of two weeks from art camp—I felt an elusive grief each time. I didn't know why my body seemed to lose sensation or I was unable to speak. There was a dense discomfort in my stomach. I thought perhaps I had defective parts, like sex didn't quite work for me. But my body knew why even when my mind hadn't put it together. When I said that in therapy, Roz told me it was a breakthrough.

Really, P.T. was the closest I ever got to feeling connected during sex. Looking back, I think it was partially because when he was turned on it consumed him so entirely that there was enough erotic energy for the both of us. He felt so sexually unencumbered, so intent on finding ways to please me, that my initial semiparalysis went unnoticed, my numbness eventually dissipated. He really wanted to turn me on, overwhelm me. He really wanted to figure out how my body reacted to the ways he touched me. I felt totally wanted, and that was enough for me. There was also something about him being so sloppy, his hair often greasy, his nails dirty, that made me feel beautiful in comparison. It surprised me that I enjoyed that feeling, but I always dressed with him in mind. That's so far away now—picking out silk button-downs and miniskirts, sheer tops and platform Mary Janes, wearing lipstick and perfume.

Even before I went no contact as an adult, Dad only called me once or twice a year at random in the middle of the afternoon, drunk or high, talking nonsense, often referring to me by my mother's name. I stopped picking up. He left me one last voicemail, around Christmastime, before he stopped trying.

It expressed unusual concern, as though he knew something about my life I didn't. *Baby, it's Dad. I'm worried about you. You seem so . . . I don't know. Anyway, New York City is beautiful this time of year. Happy holidays.* His voice sounded calm when he spoke, sober. I always liked the sound of his voice when he was sober. It had a chuckle built into it, pliable, then abrupt, like a wheel stopping fast in dry dirt. He'd say something and let it hang there. As a kid my whole body went numb when there was a certain shift in his tone of voice. My skin learned how to listen to him. My hair, my solar plexus.

Damian feels bad for him, it's why he keeps in touch. That, and he chooses to focus on who Dad was during the hours he was sober. Someone brimming with relentless, chaotic, fantastic energy—now just to the left of being a vegetable. Plus, I do remember, when Damian came out to Dad over the phone, that Dad said, "That's really cool, Dame. It's great to know who you are." It was the kindest reaction he got from any adult in our lives, and that understandably goes a long way. Especially since it was a forced coming out. He was fifteen and Mom's boyfriend at the time found gay porn on Damian's computer when he was looking up directions to a restaurant on MapQuest. He yelled out, "Fucking nasty!" and came into the kitchen, where Damian was having ice cream, to say, "Dude, what's hot about forty-year-old guys in Catholic school uniforms fucking each other's poop shoots?" Then her boyfriend started laughing, in a manner that gave away his deep discomfort. My mother turned maroon and remained silent. Damian brought it up to her later that night, while the three of us were watching TV. He started crying, which he never did, and she went cold. "Christ, it's fine, I could already tell, Damian. Just keep it to yourself for a while at school." Sure, at this point we saw our dad once every two years at best, but he accepted Damian during that defining time. I get why he wants to hold on to Dad. I get why his sadness is so big. I feel it, too, which Damian maybe doesn't pick up on. I'm calloused, but barely. Which is why I steer clear. I've come to learn that cutting off a parent is another stigma that most people don't understand. Common, sort of. Normal, no. Most people think whatever soul contract you have with them is too great to comprehend as a mortal, so you have to succumb and stay involved.

P.T. also held on to the idea that I should repair my relationship with my dad, as though my issue with him was overdramatized. P.T. never met my dad, but he asked me about him a lot. He found his own parents, who owned a restaurant supply business in New Jersey, to be offensively normal, or as he said, "banally destructive political moderates." He enjoyed the stories I would tell him about mine. He loved that my parents lived in subsidized housing when I was a kid, that they were creatives who had eccentric friends. *My childhood wasn't like* Just Kids, *if that's what you're thinking*, I said. *My parents were usually wasted and screaming. We watched a lot of TV.* But P.T. liked the character I'd made of my dad.

After I talk with Damian I go home and accidentally fall back asleep while changing my sheets, waking at noon to a bunch of missed calls and texts from Bunny. I also slept through my weekly check-in with my boss, which is not great, considering it's just about the only thing at my job I have to show up for at a particular time.

Uhhhhhhh Clarice?

HELLO?

Nicole just told me u went on a date with RICH?

Sorry no judge it's just like . . .

girl

Dude I was sleeping.

Saying yes to a date . . . Roz's idea

did u fuck

yes

about to go again

foul

i've been telling u to test drive dating for how long?

Bunny I love you but . . .

you ain't my doctor

Clearly or u'd be healed

I feel offended on behalf of Rich, who is a better man than I am. There's not a chance in hell I'm telling Bunny what we actually did. Our activities are confidential. I write to my boss to tell her my internet went out so I couldn't get on the VPN, but she responds, *All good, nothing new until next week. The higher-ups loved the holiday dildo box designs. Especially the Pinyon Script typeface!* I eat a banana and check P.T.'s Instagram, Twitter, and Google presence. No changes, but it's a nervous tic at this point, and I want to get in the zone for tonight. I want to remember every detail of his features, his interests, soak them in. I'm about to do another email deep dive to see if I can find his number somehow and try, once and for all, to do a people-finder search and see where his phone is currently registered, but am interrupted once again, this time by Hall and Oates's "Maneater," my mom's ringtone. Good god.

"You've got Clarice on the line," I say in monotone, and she launches in. Apparently she bought me a dress to wear for her wedding.

"So, the wedding is now on New Year's Day instead of Christmas Eve," Mom says, not skipping a beat.

"Wow. Kind of a big last-minute change, no?"

"Well, I can do what I want, it's at Sue's brother's new bed-and-breakfast. We're their first wedding, it isn't even officially open yet. Let me send you a little link here."

She does. Anthony's La Dolce Vita Bed & Brekki. A stunning refurbished farmhouse decorated to look neo-Roman. Lots of twinkling lights, columns, flying babies, some vague frescos, armless women.

"Oh, wow. This is themed."

"Her brother Anthony just opened it with this man he's gay with, Henry. They're very sweet. Although Anthony has gained some weight recently."

"What does that have to do with anything?" I rub my brow. "Also you don't say *he's gay with*. Henry is Anthony's partner. Or husband. Or boyfriend."

"'Partner' makes me think of law firms." She laughs.

"Or equals? You lived in Chelsea for twenty years and have a gay son, how is this news?"

"For one minute of your life, stop picking on me. And look at the next little link I sent. It's the dress for you."

"This is nice, Mom." It is.

"It's a Simone Rocha dress. Expensive, very cool. Do you know her? Irish. Not like I was going to get you a Jessica

McClintock. But I wanted you to match the theme: roses. So old it's new again, don't you agree?"

"Roses? That's a theme? What about the Roman Empire theme already present?"

"Oh, the interior columns can be removed. Those are for show. Also, I thought maybe you could fly back here early and help me pick between the wedding dresses I got. I have three I couldn't choose from, if you can believe it."

"Mom, no. I can't take the time off work."

"You work remotely, Clarice, don't think I don't know what that means."

"But the travel days . . ."

"Oh, just say you don't want to, for Christ's sake."

I'm silent for a second. "I don't want to."

She's silent for a second. "I'll ask Damian, then."

"Damian? Why don't you ask Mitch's daughter?"

I hear her feet padding down the hall, a door closes, and her voice drops to a loud hush.

"She's a drip, Clarice!" she says. "She's always complaining about her 'patellar tendonitis' like she's four hundred years old. Plus, I don't trust her eye."

"You'll figure it out, Mom," I say. She's always been shameless in asking us to participate in her love life, an expectation that has dampened not at all with age.

"Well, then, I guess I'll get all my big asks out of the way."

"Shoot."

"I want you to sing at the wedding." She giggles in glee. I, too, start laughing. "You were in choir," she says, recognizing the differences in our tone.

"No, Damian was in choir."

"Really?"

"It's a firm no, Mom."

"Right, too busy out in Hollywood to help a plebeian like me." She pauses and mutters, so I ask her to repeat herself. "I said I guess I'll ask Damian for that as well. As usual."

"I wish you all the luck in the world. I gotta go, Mom."

"One last thing! Did Damian tell you about the calls?"

"What calls?"

"The pranks I've been getting."

"Uh, no."

"Some perv has been calling and doing that heavy breathing into the phone! Like some horror film. No caller ID, of course."

"Oh, god," I say, worried this is somehow my fault. Could it be P.T.?

"Part of me is thinking it's your father." She laughs. "He's always spiritually sensed when I'm in love, you know that."

"That's creepy, Mom," I say quietly.

"Oh, of course it is, but, well, Mitch has a rifle or two, and your dad's in that wheelchair, so I'm not particularly concerned if it is him. Damian says he uses Siri to call people, but then I'm not sure how he'd get so close to the phone!"

I'm disturbed at how lighthearted, even flattered, she sounds—they've been divorced for over twenty years. Some people never let go. I keep learning that.

I hang up with her and spend hours lying still, looking at the ceiling. EDM is blasting from upstairs, but still, at one point I think I fall asleep with my eyes open. I don't want to expend too much energy before I leave for Code Red's. Who knows who or what I'll be confronting tonight. For better or worse, I need to be ready.

By sunset I'm on Sunset, driving around waiting for the strike of stakeout hour, and out of nowhere, Roz calls. Everyone's on me today, the digital age has robbed us of our solitude. Although it's probably a sign from the universe to reconsider my plans for tonight, I find it irksome.

"How have you been feeling, Clarice? I've been concerned after you canceled our last two sessions," Roz's voice comes through the speaker of my car.

"I wouldn't say great."

"Are you still thinking about P.T.?"

"Well, yes, I am. I'm still thinking about him a lot." I pull into the parking lot of the 99 Cents store off Sunset and Kingsley. Oddly not the first time I've talked to Roz from here. Phone sessions I often do in the car—sometimes doing therapy on my actual couch, looking around at my piles of unshelved books and laundry, is too much to bear.

"Have you done any more research?"

"I would say, yes, Roz. Yes, I've done some."

"More internet?"

"More internet. Nothing new since Thanksgiving Day. No information. Although, I did go back to that bar I saw him at." I hesitate, then say in a rush, "And I brought this poor fucking guy along as a fake date who ended up being a PI, which I didn't know—honestly, it was an unexpected win—but I finally talked to the bartender P.T. was flirting with."

"Oh, Clarice. Did she remember him?"

"She fucked him, in fact."

"So, she could confirm it was him?"

"Uh, not—no. She couldn't exactly."

"What do you mean?"

"Well, in some insane stroke of misfortune, she was too drunk to remember his name and she felt their connection was too far along to ask him again."

"Oh, wow. Did you tell this woman why you were asking?"

"I made up a story about him being an old study-abroad classmate who went through a recent family tragedy, but I didn't want to disturb him, yadda yadda."

"I can understand why you would do that, Clarice," Roz says slowly, and goes on to talk about how hard it is, sometimes, to make decisions when you're trying to assess danger. As she speaks, I watch a young guy coming out of the 99 Cents store, carrying in one hand a small silver Christmas tree, and in the other a gallon of bleach. The guy gets into a Hyundai sedan across from me and puts his seat belt on. He sits for a minute, looking tired, and pulls on a vape. I feel strangely like I'm looking into a mirror.

"But that's not the worst, like, part, exactly," I tell Roz after she attempts to assuage whatever guilt she thinks I might be feeling for that minor lie. "You know how I mentioned the date I took there was a former PI?"

"Yes."

"Well, that was a coincidence, obviously. A lucky one, I think, because I have more tools to attack this situation. He knows how to locate people or track them or whatever and that's what I need to do. To be safe. But Rich and I, the detective guy, we sort of, like, followed this bartender woman home because when I talked to her she said P.T. was going to come back to see her the next night. Which is tonight. So, we went there to find a spot to stake out if I wanted to watch for him. Nothing too insane, I wouldn't be confronting anyone, it would be low-key . . ." I'm talking faster than usual.

"Clarice, I want you to take a deep breath."

"Yup, breathing."

"I don't want this to sound harsh, but you seem to be struggling with impulse control. Probably because of the fear that's coming up for you. Would you say that's fair? That some compulsive behavior is getting triggered?"

"Right, sure, fair." My teeth clenched. "But if I don't figure this out, I could be the one who gets really fucked."

"Do you have a sense you're in danger?"

"Do you?"

"I see you're afraid, and I trust your intuition, but I also know this is a loaded situation."

"Right. No shit." I put my head in my hands. "Sorry, that's not directed at you."

"Clarice, honestly, I'm liking the anger I feel coming to the surface. I want to take a look at where that anger stems from. Some of it is family-of-origin stuff. You know that. But I think we need to make a game plan so we can lean away from doing anything that might feel simply guided by panic."

"What have I done that sounds 'simply guided by panic'?" I feel my adrenaline start to rise. She wants me to be in touch with my anger? She's fucking placating me. "You know he promised me that he would not go to his grave without ruining my life, right?"

"Clarice, I want to validate these feelings. And I want to stop you from turning it in on yourself."

"I need to find out if he's here, Roz. That's my most important thing right now, okay? Because I really, really think he is but I also have no actual clue."

"Yes, and I think there is a way we can find this out. Without going there. We can make a plan together."

"How?"

"There has to be someone we can reach out to who can identify his location. Perhaps your old lawyer?"

"I don't know how Jason Beranji could possibly have access to that information."

"How about this woman he was flirting with, the bartender, the woman who might be seeing him? You can tell her the truth about why you initially asked."

"Her name is Amanda." I watch the young guy in the Hyundai pull out and drive away, Juul still firmly between the lips. I swear he shoots me a knowing glance as he drives by—like he's somehow in on my situation and thinks I should stick to my plan. He's wearing sunglasses so it's impossible to really tell. I should have gotten out of the car when he was still parked and asked him for a hit of his vape.

"Well, I would tell Amanda the truth and ask her," Roz says carefully. "You laid the groundwork when you spoke to her initially. You can explain why you were reluctant to tell the whole story. She would probably want to know if a man with whom she's involved has a history of stalking and untreated mental illness. And you want to know if he's here."

I look down at my legs. I'm wearing sweatpants; there's a small brown spot, I'm pretty sure it's coffee. I remember the last time I was at her office, Roz was wearing knee-high boots. She probably is right now. My therapist dresses better than I do. Now, how does that make me feel?

"But what if he's better now?"

"Maybe he is, maybe he isn't. But if it is him, if he is here with the intention of harassing you, and he's leaving items at your house? That would worry me. Have there been more items?"

"Yeah. I mean, some trash. But honestly, Roz, if I go around interrogating women he's sleeping with and start telling them I think he's severely mentally disturbed? I don't know, I just think he would be more resolved to do something horrible to me."

"Have you reported the objects to the police?"

"No, it would be useless. They'd tell me it was a crazy neighbor."

"Do you think that's possible?"

"Why would it be?"

"Clarice, I really think we can find some solutions here. Ones that don't include you having to park outside this woman's house on the off chance that you see him. I think one thing that will be helpful, for now, is to talk this through with people close to you. I think if you shared what you're going through with Bunny, or with Damian, or maybe reach out to Maxine, it might not feel so isolating. They might be able to offer some support. And of course, me. I'm always here."

I bite the side of my cheek and mindlessly begin to fiddle with the dials and buttons of the air-conditioning. My throat tightens. Why talk to anyone? Tell anyone anything? All she and I ever do is boil my life down to how neglectful and idiotic my parents were. Did I even get that fucked over by my parents? More than the average person? Maybe I should ask Damian how he compartmentalizes, maybe there are some instructions I could follow. Ultimately, I just want Roz to fix it for me, for someone to fix it for me. I want to sign on to therapy and have her say, "Good news, Clarice! It's not him! I had my team look into it." Or better yet, "Well, Clarice, it's him, but I've gotten you set up with the witness protection program, a new wig, and a tax-free ten million dollars." Instead, the suggestion is to talk to Code Red. To clear the air with Bunny. To consider, once more, why I'm so angry at my dad. People can try to help, but there's only so much another person can do—we're alone in some things.

"Clarice?" she asks after a minute. "I hope that silence means you're reconsidering the plan."

"It does," I tell her, reconsidering. "I hear you. I'll go home."

18

There was a TV playing *Friends* reruns in the small claims court waiting room. The walls were yellow, the air frenetic. It was swarmed in there and poorly ventilated, which seemed hazardous for summer in Brooklyn. People were nervously waiting to get lucky or get fucked over for a max of five grand. A guy sitting in front of me with an open takeout container of pungent noodles knew the security guard by name. I'd never been to a racetrack, but I imagined a similar atmosphere.

I didn't want to admit it to myself at the time, but Jason Beranji, Esq., seemed just as nervous as I was when we arrived, if not more so. Both of us kept looking over to the door to see if P.T. had walked in. Jason asked if I had any water.

"No, only coffee, but I have some Klonopin," I told him.

"What's that?" He took off his suit coat, pit stains revealed.

"It's a benzo. It makes you feel calm. But not super fucked if you just have one once in a while."

"Are they legal?" he asked, using the sleeve of the coat to pat down his face.

"Yeah."

"Sure, why not?"

I reached into my purse for the pill bottle, took two out, kept one for me and handed one to Jason. He asked for a sip of my coffee to swallow.

"Jason, not that it matters at this point," I said after a moment. "But is this your first time at court?"

"No, no, no. Fourth time. Second time without my dad. But that last one I did was just a biker getting hit by a car door opening."

"Right."

We waited inside the courtroom during the trial just before us, I suppose to be locked and loaded and waste no time. The case we got to witness was a dispute between a woman named Kay, looking a little worse for the wear, and her former boss and owner of a local Tex-Mex restaurant, Marfie, who read immediately as airtight and vindictive. Apparently, Kay got fired for being fifteen minutes late to a shift, so she decided to camp outside the restaurant one morning and scream that Marfie put lotion in the breakfast tacos.

"It's a lie! I whip sour cream into the eggs!" Marfie said.

"Well, it gives people the runs," said Kay. Jason and I looked down, both stifling laughter.

Marfie was trying to get $2,500 in what she believed to be lost sales due to false claims and disturbance of the peace. She also would be filing for a protective order so Kay could no longer come within a one-mile radius of the restaurant. The judge told her, in legal jargon, good luck with the order, but she wasn't going to make Kay pay Marfie squat. So, there is justice, I thought to myself.

By the time we were called to the stand, P.T. still hadn't shown up. Jason clenched his fist and raised it when we were called and he wasn't there, as though we'd achieved some kind of victory.

"We consider this a win?" I asked.

"I like to stay positive," Jason said.

After small claims court, Jason and I texted maybe once every ten days. He wanted to make sure P.T. hadn't contacted me and that we were "still on" for the trial, which was months away. Like I was shopping around for other lawyers? I could barely open my curtains. *Yes, Jason, we're still on.* Once he sent the emoji of a guy in robes with a gavel.

As for P.T., he hadn't come near me or contacted me since the emails he sent over the weekend in April, before the second court order was delivered to him. Not in any way I could prove. None of his normal emails or letters, none of his calls. He didn't contact any of my family or friends. He was not spotted outside of any buildings. It was positive but also agitating. His absence was noted daily. It hovered. A forced legal boundary. More like a constant reminder of potential danger.

Still, over the previous few months, I'd gotten two strange pieces of mail I could only assume were from him. They were white envelopes with my name and address in Comic Sans type. No return address. Postmarked from Manhattan. If it was him, which it had to be, it seemed the blank page folded crisply inside held a tacit understanding that he was sending the exact message he'd been sending for months. He knew at this point, I could write his letters myself.

When Maxine witnessed me open the second one, she got pissed, kicked the couch, and said we should get them fingerprinted. I thought about it but didn't have the strength. I woke up with a snap in the middle of the night, afraid that perhaps the second letter was sprinkled with anthrax or some other invisible, lethal substance. I spent the night googling slow-acting poisons. When I told Jason, he, too, suggested forensics.

I had another unnerving encounter when I ran into an old coworker from the creative agency at the bodega near my house. I was picking up some fried chicken, one of the few adventures I took, and there was Benji, a graphic-designing skater boy who hung out at LES bars and dated women he would forget to introduce at the Christmas parties. He spoke loudly and had the Ken-doll face of an asshole.

"As I live and fucking breathe, Clarice. How have you been doing?"

"Just, you know, WFH," I said to him, suddenly shoving my hair behind my ears and pulling my hat down.

"You never responded to my text inviting you to my birthday party, Clarice. Saucy behavior. I thought you died until I saw you on Tinder!" He tilted his chin up at the guy behind the counter as a deli hoagie was passed to him. I felt a lurch of panic. The idea of fried chicken now seemed practically perverse.

"I'm not on Tinder, Benji," I told him as the bodega began to spin. "I've never been on Tinder."

"You are though, dude, I screenshotted it because I thought it was . . . a weird account. Look," he said, taking out his phone and scrolling. "Maybe you made an account when you were plastered or something."

It was a photo of my face, indeed it was. But it was my LinkedIn photo and my bio read "Ruiner" and had the blood-drop emoji next to it. Benji said there were two or three photos, but that was the only one he'd screenshotted. I knew it was P.T. I was instantly reminded of a passive threat in one of his letters: *I know every inch of you. Think of all the nude pictures I will always have.*

"You're being used as a catfish, dude," he said. "It happened to my cousin. So fucked."

I asked him to text the photo to me. He gave me a hug and I could see him scrutinizing my chin breakout when he gave me one last look goodbye. I immediately sent the screenshot to Bunny, who told me to send her the sunshine emoji as a symbol when I was ready and she would buy me a one-way ticket to Los Angeles. I sent her the black hole emoji. *You joke*, she said, *but he'd be a nonissue. He couldn't find u in Cali.*

19

I can't tell anyone I'm outside Code Red's house except for Rich, whom I did tell. I saw the three texting dots appear and then disappear a few times. That was about an hour ago.

I tried to talk myself out of coming here after that conversation with Roz. Her suggestion was to go home and get some rest, and I thought about doing that for at least twenty minutes. Instead I said fuck it, got an iced coffee, and drove here to wait for P.T.

I run through a variety of scenarios both bad and worse in my head. Code Red and P.T. approach me with a police officer; they tell me they have footage of me and Rich loitering outside. Code Red and P.T. chloroform me from behind as I try to peek into her living room. I figure out it's not P.T., just as I fall into Code Red's backyard cedar hot tub, knock my temple at a bad angle, and drown. Then the worst. I watch P.T. watch me through a window as he fucks an unsuspecting Code Red; then later he finds me and kills me.

I know that whether or not I see him tonight, I don't have a plan. I also know I should probably abort mission, take a pill, and sleep for upward of three months. When I catastrophize, Bunny says things to me like *Tell them it's going to be okay* and points to my head, like there's a group of demons in there who have risen and taken the helm. It's patronizing but not incorrect. As I see it, this is the fastest way between two points, knowing and not knowing.

I'm about three cars down across the street from Code Red's house. Rich told me to set myself back a bit from the driveway, it will put me at an angle to see his face when he gets out of his car, and my car, which he may or may not know the make and model of, won't be the first thing he sees when he walks out the door. Even if he knows my car, if he's not looking for it and he's distracted by imminent fucking, the likelihood that he clocks me at a distance is near to none.

I've been here since seven thirty, although I know most fucking doesn't happen until at least nine. I'm almost offended when, ten minutes later, he swings confidently, roughly, into the driveway, I heard him before I saw the car. *Democracy Now!* blasting. All four windows are down. Very P.T. He hates all media outlets, finds them untrustworthy with inadequate prose, but he always had news on full blast at every hour. It's how he woke up.

He sits in the car for a moment, and I wish at this point that I were closer so I might catch a glimpse of what he's doing. He gets out, wearing the same bomber as the other night, but a hoodie underneath with the hood up. His head is down, looking at his phone. He walks around and leans on the hood of his car, likely letting her know he's there. At this point, fear temporarily gone, to get a better look, I slither over to the passenger seat and quietly open the door. I peek out behind the back of a Honda HR-V. Thank god I do, because P.T. walks around to the other side of the car to get a backpack out of the back seat, and although I still don't get a direct look at his face, I see from a distance, thanks to her garden track lights, a large black shape on the back of his left hand. The coyote tattoo.

I actually gasp and I swear his head jerks in my direction, but thankfully, the front door opens to reveal Code Red in a silk sheath mini. It's baby blue and pulls at the hips and breasts too tightly, stretching the fabric awkwardly even from a distance, making the whole thing sexier. Her hair is large and free.

He moves forward at her and their bodies collide; she puts her hands above her head as he hugs her, their silhouette briefly looking like a two-headed bug. The door closes, and I imagine, or remember, his hands grabbing her (my) ass, as she (I) jumps up and wraps around him, legs around his waist, crotch bumping against his belly as he walks her (me) to some surface to decide which orifice he will descend upon.

I let about five minutes pass, my heart beating, my eyes juiced with the numbing impact of adrenaline. But this is it, it's my time now. I remember Rich's instructions for car-searching. Look at the condition of the car's exterior, at the plates, at what's on it, stickers, both official and entertaining. What's inside, how clean is it, how far the seat is pulled up. Don't analyze the data, he said, just take inventory. At first, everything will seem like it does or does not point in the direction you want it to point, he told me. *Observe* now, deduce later. Do nothing rash. In fact, do nothing.

I painfully crouch-walk on the asphalt over to the car, which has New Jersey plates. I immediately interpret. P.T. never had a car when we were together, but his parents live in an unexpectedly beautiful and rural part of Jersey, so if he got one, it would have been from them. If he decided to leave New York, he would have driven. To see America. Or rather, her bars. Probably with a big duffel bag, the guitar he played badly, and a few boxes of books.

There are no stickers on the back of this car; the registration seems up to date. I put the license plate number in my notes app. On the back seat, driver's side, there is a wide-open Target bag with an empty package of Haribo gummy bears and an opened pack of Hanes men's underwear. Size L. He was bigger than that when we were together. This version of him seems to have lost fifteen to twenty pounds. Which is too bad, really—his size was sexy and imposing.

In the front, on the passenger seat, is a book I can't see the title of because its cover is half obscured by a sweatshirt on top of it. I do see, on the bottom part of the spine that pokes out, however, that it says "PraxisHaus." Analyze later—but P.T. is not only a fan but in fact briefly worked for this niche, intelligentsia publishing house when he was in college. One of the last gifts I gave him was a book they published. *Listen Harder: The Erotics of Psychotherapy*.

I told myself that after looking at his car and seeing him enter the house I would leave. I would digest the information, then I would speak to Code Red honestly when I had more of a leg to stand on. I could buck up and tell her the truth about our history. After sleeping with him again, surely she would know his name. But the book and the New Jersey license plates give me a dizzying need to know more. I could find out right now. I could just get a better look inside, right now, and I would know.

The living room is dark. I crouch forward toward the gate to the back, where I am met with the reality of a tall, literal white picket fence surrounding her backyard. Which means I have to crawl through some bushes and enter from the neighbor's backyard to get to the tree that Rich mentioned had a vantage point to the second-floor windows. The hedges are tight but there's an opening at the bottom. In the first of many more humbling moments to come, I'm sure, I crawl on my knees, dirty my jeans, and get ready to climb.

The tree is a real mighty magnolia, those famous Los Angeles beauties with roots that look like hardened veins. Early December, it's filled not with blossoms but with those browning pods that I suppose will one day be flowers. I spot one relatively sturdy, low-hanging branch, one that will get me behind a large shield of brown-green gleaming leaves, but also close enough to see directly into a window with a light on that has no curtains. I heave myself up, climb, and straddle my stakeout spot victoriously. It's at that moment I realize I can already hear them. They wasted no time, and the window I see is both to her room and open. It's nice in there, very tasteful, nothing on the walls except for a large mirror above her bed with opulent antique trim, which makes it so I can see her in a kind of camel's pose: dangling hair, the reflection of her neck, chin, collarbone, and freckled breasts, nearly translucent pink nipples the size of small cookies. I know she's sitting on his face, rocking her hips back and forth on his warm, virtuosic mouth. He's still got all his clothes on, I'm sure, although I can't see him. I become, despite myself, mildly aroused, and quite gently, involuntarily, buck my hips as she does, on the hard branch of this tree. I feel my stomach lurch. Her noises. Her noises are begging, desirous, come deep from the throat. Code Red releasing some kind of primal, calcified stress. He's barely audible. I know she's putting on no act. I'd sit over him like that often. He'd bite my thighs in tiny, restrained nips, trace his fingers over the crotch of my underwear, tease but not open the elastic edge near my inner leg, and I wanted him to start so badly it actually made me angry—sad even—and eventually when he did, after what felt like so, so long, sometimes I'd tear up. *Torture can be so pleasurable*, he told me, insufferably. *I think we both know that.*

Maybe that's all this is. Continued torture. Somehow pleasurable. But I'm overwhelmed, and now remembering I'm not the hugest fan of heights and the precarious nature of my position has me feeling trapped. Needing to pee, with a growing sense of vertigo, the rough bump on a branch of a magnolia bud digging into my sciatica, all while listening to some guy who is almost definitely P.T. pleasure another woman. P.T., who seems to be doing just fine. Still alive, writing poetry, still fucking, still drinking and flirting in bars, reading his overripe art theory books. I want to find him there. I don't want to find him there. That both things are still true continues to confuse me. Fuck, what if it's like what Bunny said at the beach: *Some kind of emotional version of how rape victims sometimes masturbate to the memory of rape?* It happens, it's normal, it's a survival mechanism. You need to connect to what happened somehow, get something out of it.

I think of my mom, when she told me about being raped as a teenager. She'd never shared it with anyone before. I must have been sixteen at the time, and because she was drunk and I was stoned and having a bad high, I didn't want her to be telling me the story. Not like that, after dinner, casually, with an unnaturally tight smirk on her face, her cheekbones and forehead bursting through the skin. But I couldn't speak. I just had a paralytically stoned but cogent thought as she spoke, a thought I've had many times since: *Her rape is my true dad.* Not the rapist, whoever the fuck that rotting incubus was, but the rape itself. Experiences like that become the bloodline.

It's a horrible thought, horrible story, but here it is. Her mother, my nonie, set her up on a date with a twenty-eight-year-old businessman whom Nonie had sat next to at a restaurant. The two of them got to talking—flirting really—and Nonie told him that although she was married, her beautiful daughter wasn't. He should take her out. The next day, he showed up at the house to pick up my mom before she even knew about the date. My teenage mother, home from her senior year at an all-girls boarding school, who loved Herman's Hermits, who played chess, made red clay pinch pots, collected dead butterflies and beetles to polyurethane and frame, was out by the pool, eating a cucumber and butter sandwich. She had moments earlier gotten her period in her new terry cloth one-piece and ruined the crotch. Nonie told her she had fifteen minutes to dress because a man was taking her to dinner. My mom went inside and chose a poplin sheath with matching pumps. She was excited. She'd never been on a proper date before.

This guy was a nouveau riche suit, my mother told me, with, *ugh*, wet blond curls, and a '69 Rolls-Royce Silver Shadow that looked like a hearse. He didn't even take her out to dinner; he said he forgot to make a reservation. He just took her to his house, a mansion with more hideous sculptures around than furniture. "You're a collector?" she asked. "I'm an investor," he responded. Gave her white wine with ice. Ritz crackers and dips, cut fruit. Food you'd feed to a baby. Eventually, and with unexpected strength, he pushed her onto a deep-seated velvet couch. He didn't notice she was wearing a menstrual belt. Or that her eyes were squeezed shut and her stomach jerking. The only witnesses were the fallen orange evening and a glass statue of a centauress. She said she went home and took a bath, so scared she was going to get pregnant she opened her legs and let the water torrent from the faucet into her vagina.

No one is born knowing how to transmute violence, so she swallowed it quietly and it transmuted her. In ways that now seem filmic, cliché. (Although what diminishes someone's pain more efficiently than calling it cliché?) It changed the kind of teenager she was. It changed her interests (she lost most of them), her concentration (couldn't finish a book or movie), the kind of people she dated from then on (mean losers), her plentiful appetite (gone), and her sleep cycles (troubled). "I was totally sheltered," she told me, "then, snap, I was a jaded bitch." That one night, that one guy, his unfortunate ability to pin her down.

To this day I wonder what would have happened if she had told someone back then, which is what people always say to do. Even though that only works out a scant percentage of the time. Prescriptive, mostly unhelpful, half advice is: *Tell someone.* And whatever, who the fuck am I, but I do wonder, and I do wish she had. I want to go back in time and tell her to do so. *Tell someone. Tell someone. Tell someone.* Tell someone so the shame will only maybe try to kill you instead of probably try to kill you. No guarantees it will help, too many people are emotionally and morally incompetent, or just similarly untaught, but try anyway, and speak slowly, all the details, with, yes, again, the often vain hope that this person will help you, get you medical attention, will not punish, ignore, or doubt you but will react with kindness and a wise, firm plan of action, so you can feel what it's like to have someone carry part of an undue burden for you, one that shouldn't be yours, but is, and will be going forward. It might alleviate some of the dread in your bowels, sitting like a carcass that lets out a weak bit of stink each time you speak. Then you might find a way to treat some of the sickness it gave you. Incurable but treatable. Tell someone so you can stay with your boyfriend, courteous age-appropriate Greg, instead of breaking up with him to briefly date the rapist because you understandably, half-unconsciously, shifted the narrative from "rape" to "a man's confused enthusiasm" to cause the least amount of damage to your own psyche. You might avoid the string of scumbags that will follow him, including Dad. This sounds like blaming you, but I'm not. It was your mother, all eyes on marriage, pushing you into a horrible situation. It was one sleazy man's damage causing more damage. You had no part in those things—but it's possible it catalyzed the years of comically questionable decisions that followed. I want to know what could have made it better for you, softened the ache, changed the course. Better yet, I'd like to know what could have prevented you from being alone in that house with that guy in the first place, or prevented me, for that matter, from being situated in a tree outside P.T.'s lover's house, 99.5 percent sure that this man followed me across the country, at best to presently taunt me, at worst to murder me. Maybe I would be somewhere else right now. Or maybe I wouldn't.

My daze lifts and I snap from my thoughts when I clock Code Red looking directly out the window, squinting a little. I can see her putting together that what she is looking at is a face. Her expression goes from confused to panicked, which makes me panic, too. She starts to say something to P.T.—who is still below her, his face is still not visible to me—and I duck fast, smacking my forehead squarely into a neighboring branch, enough that it makes me instantly ill, my vision momentarily gone snowy. I reach out for a branch to balance just as I realize that there's nothing for me to grab. I fall forward and all limbs begin to scramble, my body attempting to hold or stop or gain some kind of traction on branches or trunk, desperate to ease my fall into a sudden, hard, unfortunate heap. I want to yell but keep my mouth shut. I feel a burning scrape on the side of my face and can already sense blood rising from a cut on my cheek, bountiful and hot like a mocking cackle of laughter. Oh, what a mark it will leave. I expect someone to yell at me, for Code Red to figure out I'm not in her yard but the yard next door and come rushing in with threats that the authorities are en route. But I look out at the grass and into the street, the one lamp laying a dusty yellow over the cars, and I am met with the relative quiet of distant traffic, and the ocean sound coming from the proximity of my ear to the dirt. I lie there for a while, in part because I am afraid I'll find out I can't use one of my limbs. At one point a woman walks slowly by on the sidewalk, squinting her eyes toward my body from a distance, and asks if I am okay. I tell her I am meditating. She says, "Good for you."

By the time I finally stand up to walk, my head bowed in disgrace, I've come to a dreadful, dizzy peace with the fact that I'm probably going to get caught. But when I get to the edge of the neighbor's yard, what I find instead is P.T.'s car peeling out of the driveway next door, speeding down the road, leaving an echo on an otherwise silent street.

20

I honestly cannot remember those two days of the actual trial in much more than bits, some parts very clearly, others gone. For hours before it began I sat on my bed, waiting to walk down to the court. I was exhausted, didn't sleep, and the trial wasn't until 2 p.m. What are you supposed to do beforehand? Go to yoga? Run a few errands? Whatever I ate, I didn't digest, it sat in my stomach, so I didn't eat anything, I just drank blue Gatorade. The very fact that it was in walking distance felt cruel. I could have been going to the farmer's market. A movie theater where you can also order lunch. Junior's for cheesecake. Nope. Court. Every time: the security line, the elevators, the pews, the waiting. Observing my compatriots. Their clothes, their facial expressions, their posture, their class. That brittle air. The minute one crossed the threshold, one's skin became chalky, aged. I was still surprised by how everything was just to the left of grand-looking—as if a cathedral had been stripped of its reason for worship. Jason had brought his dad that day. Roberto Beranji. "Two Beranjis for the price of one!" he said when he sat down. The sum of Beranji Squared. I suppose it should have given me pause, because it meant he wasn't sure he could close, so to speak. But I couldn't form many thoughts, with cotton for brains, crackling arid mouth. And I did feel safer sitting on those pews with two large New York lawyers of middling intelligence on either side of me. P.T. sat down behind us with his court-appointed lawyer, a guy with knobby knuckles in a muted suit. Like last time, P.T. made noisy attempts to get my attention. His hair was grown out. His face looked like he had lost weight, but his body didn't. He was wearing a plaid shirt tucked in. He wanted me, so badly, to look him right in the eyes.

The same question arises in a situation particularly good or bad. *How did I end up here?* Part of the pain is the chance factor, the fact that life could have gone in infinite other directions. P.T. quoted Simone Weil when I was upset with him: "*All flaws are the same. Incapacity to feed on light.*" That was both of our problems, wasn't it?

I had little bruises and fingernail marks from where I grabbed on anxiously to my arms. They called us in. I saw the face of a male judge with a neatly trimmed raven mustache raised on the stand before us. Expressionless. I remembered what Jason had said about hoping for a female judge. I heard Beranji Sr. let out a displeased groan.

The sound of the trial was the sound of the adults in *Peanuts* cartoons. Wah-wah-wah-wah. I could think of little other than how thirsty I continued to be. My face and throat, itchy with thirst. My whole body, a dehydrated headache. Had I ever tasted water in my life? I spoke much less than P.T. spoke, or than the Beranjis, both dressed in wrinkled linen.

I was sitting behind the table on the prosecutor's side of the room. P.T. went up "on the bench," in front of me. Really it was just a table. Things are just a smidge more casual in family court, it seemed. He was on one side and Jason stood opposite him, gleaming, white-pink as a cut of uncooked pork. Sweating again. I wondered if he'd sweated this much during his wedding proposal, and I hoped, for her sake, he hadn't. P.T. handed Jason a paper that Jason showed me briefly. A printout that showed our last text exchange, my words circled.

"Wow. I mean, I can't see how this would act in your favor,

sir. Can you tell me—what does that say?" Jason asked, then continued before P.T. could speak. "This right here is the last thing she ever sent directly to you, four months before she moved for an order."

"It says she doesn't want to be in contact." P.T. slit his eyes. "*Right now.*"

As though the shape and sound of the words were cut in glass. P.T. went on. "*Right now* doesn't mean forever. It doesn't even mean she won't talk tomorrow. It means *right now.* It means *right now*, in the present."

Jason said to P.T. not so under his breath: "Okay, buddy." An objection was called by both P.T. and his lawyer. It was sustained.

Jason put up his hands in surrender, asked P.T. why he continued trying to get to me so relentlessly after I told him to stop, after other people told him to stop. Jason asked him how much clearer I could have been. He said it was no secret that I was afraid. Judge Canalejo looked at me with what seemed to be a skeptically raised brow.

P.T. said he loved me and the judge nodded his head slowly but noticeably. P.T.'s eyes lowered to the table, his shoulders curled so pitifully forward they almost touched. He said I didn't understand him. No one here seemed to understand that he was trying to communicate lovingly, he said, and everyone in his life thought I was not only playing a sick game with him, but I was also mentally ill. Also he had wanted the rest of his stuff back.

Like usual, he made attempts to get my attention. I could tell without even looking at him. He must have thought the judge wouldn't realize he was trying to signal to me, or, if he got me to look over and interact, that I would seem less credible. I imagined his face cycling through expressions like one of those emotions charts for kids in a doctor's office: worry, sadness, confusion, boredom. I turned my head even more so as not to see him, but then I got this wave of rage, had a flashing impulse to run over and punch some teeth out.

Jason asked if P.T. had brought any evidence that I might want to continue some kind of exchange with him. Anything I may have sent him back. But I had sent him nothing.

I handed evidence to Jason from our folder. The letters, some emails. These ridiculous printouts of comments on my friends' Instagram posts. Facebook messages to Bunny. An email he sent to Damian. Pictures of the gifts. The judge barely glanced at them. Beranji Jr. stood and talked, talked, talked, and I shook my legs, unable to think anything except for: *Thirsty, still so thirsty.* I tried to summon and swallow spit. I could feel the dryness start to eat at the collagen in my cheeks, to suck my eyes deeper into the sockets. The overhead lighting was siphoning my spirit, bleaching me out.

Jason asked P.T. what he expected would happen after I told him to stop so many times, after my brother, Damian Dahl, an RPA operator in the Air National Guard, mind you, told him to stop, and my friends, too. P.T. sputtered. Rage beneath the desperation. The tireless repetition. *She's lying. Unwell. I don't know why. Her trauma, I understand that. I'm in love with her. This experience is ruining my life. I tried to volunteer at an elderly home but I couldn't pass the background check. To heal, I'm trying to heal. Thousands of dollars in therapy. In takeout! I used to cook. No longer. My health is declining.*

At some point Jason moved on to what we thought was our slam dunk.

"She intended to drop the order last April, which is why she didn't attend the hearing. She wanted this to be over. But when there was no order in place the defendant sent my client thirteen emails in two days. He sued her in small claims court for reasons still unclear to me, then didn't show up. He also said he could see that she was reading the emails—"

"No, no, no. Stop right there," P.T.'s lawyer interrupted,

to no objection. He stood in front of the table where I was sitting, hunched, and blocked my view of the judge. "Now, what you've just laid out here is a scenario that would seem to work favorably for your client but technically cannot be used as evidence in this trial. Let me explain here. He sent those emails over the weekend, yes? After she didn't show up to their second scheduled court date. But by that time, technically, Clarice had already gotten *another* restraining order, correct?"

I chewed my bottom lip as I listened until I felt the warm penny taste of blood.

"Yes, exactly, she went back the same day as the appointed court date because he immediately contacted her, asking her to meet in private," Jason shot back. The judge asked me directly why I didn't show up that day in the first place. I opened my mouth but Jason answered.

"She didn't want to see him! She thought the order had worked and wanted to be done with it." I could only see the back of his head, but Jason's voice was practically pleading. Beranji Sr. coughed a little and Jason took a breath.

"She wanted it to be over. She thought it was over. Then she went back to court that very day for another order when it was clear it wasn't. In this first email to her that day he had implored her to meet in private."

"Well." P.T.'s lawyer drew out the word. He paced a little, still in front of where I sat, as though he were trying to hide me from the judge. Out of the corner of my eye, I could see P.T. bouncing his knee. He always did that, even at a dinner table, he seemed not to notice that other people could feel the shaking. "What I'm saying is that anything he sent over the following weekend, quite technically, would be a violation of the order she got on Friday. Which is not why we're here."

"Your Honor, we do not know whether or not he was aware of the new order at that time," Jason said as he took a seat next to me again, wiping his palms on his suit pants.

"Yes, but the temporary order was in place," said P.T.'s lawyer. "And since the sheriff's office left him a note on the door, we can't prove my client didn't know."

"I will say, either way doesn't work well in his favor," Jason shot back. "You think it looks good if he knew about the new temporary order and then sent that many emails to my client?"

"Well, again, a *violation* of the temporary restraining order *isn't* why we're here today is all I'm saying. We are here because she wants to obtain a longer-term order *for the future*. We can't prove what he knew one way or another that weekend. We would have to come back on a different day through a different claim in order to process a violation."

Apparently the judge agreed. It was confusing to me and seemed like his own lawyer was trying to imply that it's possible he did something worse than just harass me that weekend, that he might have also violated the new restraining order. It seemed like nonsense. But he heard it, the judge heard Jason say thirteen emails. He heard about small claims. Jason had talked about how things couldn't be unheard. All I could notice was how every time P.T. spoke, the judge continued to nod in understanding like an audience member at a poetry reading.

We broke for a snack. We came back. All in, how many hours were we in there? Three or four? It seemed like I'd never not been there. This could be worse, I told myself, sipping a lukewarm Diet Coke they let me bring. Think of the murders, the purpling bruises, the little kids sitting on the benches, clutching their consolation-prize stuffed animals beside their fatally depleted parents.

In the midst of all that, I wondered if P.T. noticed what weariness had done to my face. I wondered if he still thought I was pretty. When the talking stopped, the judge left the room. He seemed to return immediately. No need for deliberating, which, coupled with the nodding, felt like a bad sign. Nerves were bursting at intervals in my body, vulgar firecrackers.

Would I have to come back to court to do this again? Could I come back to do this again? It didn't seem possible. I would die if I had to come back to this court to try again, surely my mind would give out, or at least my body. I became aware for the first time that day that I was the only woman in the room. This odd collection of men, making decisions, speaking for me.

The first actual date we went on, P.T. and I got coffee and hung out in Central Park. Sat on stairs watching teen ribbon dancers practice a routine. He briefly placed his hand on my knee without looking at me. We decided to walk down Manhattan, just as the sun started setting. Fifty-some blocks and I remember no smell, no sound. Like we had picked up on a conversation we'd started years earlier. I knew him already, I knew the inflections of his voice and his gait. I told him he seemed familiar. He said that was because we'd done drugs together. Then he told me I seemed familiar, too.

On the Lower East Side, near the Bowery, we went into a garden where people had made sculptures out of recycled wires. All of them poorly executed and seemingly influenced by hallucinogens. One was a set of angel wings. I asked him if he believed in guardian angels—walking among us, talking thoughts into our ears. He looked at me like I was dumb and said, "Of course."

We ate Mexican food well past midnight, the only people in a bright café booming ranchera. He told me about a book he wanted to write. I told him about my job. He moved my water glass to make way for my tacos. We had a few beers. He hovered his hand at my back guiding me through the door as we left. He gave me his coat outside. He took my jaw in his hand and brought the tip of his tongue across my lips. That exact feeling, that's what causes it all. That's why our nerve endings register as emotions, why and how we keep the species going.

"Can you not see how distressed she is?" the judge asked, looking P.T. square in his eyes, right before he read a guilty verdict. At the start of this, we—meaning the Beranjis and I—asked for an order of protection to be put in place for two years as a result of harassment in the second degree and stalking in the fourth degree. But the judge upped it. Harassment in the first degree, stalking in the second.

I felt the tiniest swell of relief in my chest. Then emptiness. I had been legally given what I was already due. Space and the greater possibility of peace. I watched and was repulsed by the long hug the Beranji men shared, drunk on a fresh win. I got up and gathered my things. "You're a glutton for punishment," P.T. said behind me on the way out. "You're a masochist." I felt almost surprised to see him there when I turned around to look at him, blankly in the eye, for the first time since the trial began. One of the court officers stepped between us, so P.T. raised his voice. "This is not over by a fucking long shot," he said to my back. "This isn't over. I'll wait until this runs out, Clarice. I'll find you."

I said nothing. Jason did, while rushing me out of there. Something about good luck. A little over a month later I booked a ticket to California.

21

I dart toward my own car when P.T.'s car is just barely out of sight and I drive like a maniac. I'm behind but luckily I spot his car minutes later pulling out from a gas station on Fountain and Vermont, landing him directly in front of me. He's waited for me there. I can see him readjust his rearview mirror, and to the best of my ability, I look right at him. This could be his way of asking me to follow him. I don't know. Perhaps confrontation, as he's asked for all along, is the only way for this to be resolved. Now it's what both of us want. And if he doesn't actually know I'm behind him, then at least I'll know where he lives. That evens the score some.

From Fountain he takes a right on Kingsley, my street. I swallow hard. So it is him, and yes, he knows where my apartment is. He brakes, for just a beat, right in front of my house. I think about calling the cops, calling Bunny, Rich, Damian, even Valentini, someone. My phone is on 8 percent.

I notice his turn signal go on, and when he reaches Sunset, he turns right to circle back, pulling into a nearby Del Taco. I creep behind him into the drive-thru line. I order a single chicken taco al carbon, and when I pull up to the first window to pay, I lean a little too far out the car window toward the teen cashier.

"You didn't happen to get that guy's name, did you?"

"What guy? What?"

"That guy ahead of me, his name?"

"No?" The teen is wearing a sweatshirt that has the Nike swoosh but says "Freak" on it. I eye P.T.'s car as he pauses at the exit and for once in my life I am grateful for the maddening traffic endeavor that is an LA left turn.

"You didn't peek at the credit card maybe?" I ask one more time.

He gives me a dubious, judgmental look, one that indicates I will soon be talked about and laughed at. I shake my head, pay. I'm suddenly starving and decide to hastily unwrap and take a bite—I get half taco, half wrapper. I spit and out flies a bit of chewed meat onto the dash, just as I press the gas too hard to closely follow his left turn, my tires screeching, the rest of the taco falling into my lap. Bad time to multitask.

I tail him far down Sunset until he finally takes a right turn onto a residential street. I pause as I watch him pull into the driveway and into a covered parking shed for a two-story house, numbered and clearly split into more than one residence. People are annoyed that I'm just idling in the street, multiple aggressive honks. The light goes on at the ground floor, the left-hand unit. After I clock his location within the building, I take another loop around the block. Then another, another—finding a parking spot four long blocks away. Fucking hell. When I reach his block, I duck toward his apartment and notice his car is no longer parked in the spot when I reach the house. I look behind me, suddenly wondering if he's now parked somewhere, watching. He's teasing me.

I hide briefly behind some trash cans, then duck and walk low toward the apartment parking structure. The spot where his car was parked is marked "Apt. A." I look around and see no cameras anywhere, so I move farther into the backyard. It's dark with only a bit of light coming back from the streets and it smells vaguely of dog shit. Small, yellowing patches of grass. A rusted bike is chained to a stairwell that leads to a basement.

On the first floor, P.T.'s lights are out now, but lucky for me,

I see there's a window to his unit being held ajar by a hardback thesaurus. I come closer. Next to it on the sill is an ashtray. P.T. stopped smoking when we were together (an agitated three months) after his grandpa died of heart failure, but he smoked pot occasionally. He used to roll his own; these were the filters he used. Though one of them, like Code Red gave to me, is a clove.

Without much thought, I heave the window up. I've come this fucking far and he's asking for it. In a way, on a different timeline, we do know each other well enough for me to go into his house unannounced. My limbs are shaking. I feel a pang in my eyes and the mild taste of metal, a migraine coming. My body does that, acts out at the wrong moment when tension gets to a breaking point. I always hold on too tight. P.T. used to say that he could tell my body resisted him even when I wanted him. *I go in there and it's like a vise grip. Already flinched. My little bunny, born by a shooting range.* I feel what he means. The first time I had sex with him was in the middle of the day, in his kitchen. I'd never had sex with someone for the first time both sober and in the daylight, so I was having trouble getting out of my head. I didn't tell him that, instead I said I was kind of shy and that it took me time to get turned on. I was sitting on the counter. He put his hands on either of my knees and looked me straight in the eyes. I could feel the bottom of my stomach unravel; my heart started to pound. I felt his thumbs along the interior of my knees. He asked me questions about things I liked, I suppose to distract me, kindly, because he must have felt how nervous I was. Not just things I liked in sex, things I liked in general, like movies and books. I started talking about William Carlos Williams's *Spring and All*, how my math teacher in high school gave it to me, then about this Korean teen drama I was watching at the time. Every now and then his fingers would get a little farther up my leg. He placed my hair behind my ears. Eventually he got on his knees, gently moving his tongue and lips over the crotch of my underwear until I was lightly kicking my heel against the cupboards, wanting him to take off my underwear but not having the voice to ask, and every time I tried to do it myself he stopped me. Eventually he did, pulled the crotch aside and just entered, and I came almost immediately and kept coming, which is not something I experienced before or since.

Now I am trembling and paralyzed in the middle of his living room, my heart slamming against my ribs. I do the thing Roz tells me to do when I'm dissociating: locate myself in the room, name the objects. There's a standing piano, which is strange, but P.T. always had shit in his place that didn't make sense. At his apartment in Brooklyn, he had a totem pole of Alvin and the Chipmunks and a broken accordion. Cheap stuff he found on Craigslist or on the side of the road. Here, there are boxes piled on top of each other, all unpacked. There's a huge frame, leaning against the wall, still wrapped in brown paper. Should I unwrap it? See if I recognize the artwork? It's so P.T. that he'd be here for a while now and still be living like this. Feels like an extension of his harassment, all these ways to have me get as little information as possible at every turn, even right here, inside his apartment. I'm sort of annoyed that it's a pretty nice place, about two times the size of mine. Maybe his dad died—I know he had a little nest egg coming his way at some point.

I pick up a pillow on the couch and sniff; they're new, smell like Target. I see a small pine tree in a pot covered in red foil, the type of Christmas tree you'd get at a grocery store, and a pang of longing hits me in the heart. We're all just little children, aren't we? I go into the bathroom. Sparse. Almond Dr. Bronner's, some Aveda curls shampoo. Colgate, a toothbrush, a razor. No prescriptions. All stuff he uses—although the Aveda is an upgrade. I go into his bedroom and sit on the bed. A box spring and a nice mattress, dark blue sheets and a duvet, unmade. Still no bed frame. Next to the bed on a small wooden night table is a bio of Chekhov and a pack of rolling tobacco. Inside the nightstand are a vibrator and a pack of Magnums. He hated wearing condoms. I take his pillow and though my stomach drops before I do it, I sniff in. Smells of new sheets, dirty hair, and a mild musk. But the musk is his. The nose remembers. It's his smell.

That's all the ID I need, really, but I try to look around for any piece of mail, just something that has his name on it. I'm reminded again of when he sent me a subscription to *Bride* magazine, to *Family Life* magazine, addressed to both of us with his last name, at my address. I look inside the pockets of a blue bomber, almost exactly the same as the brown one. A cap to an IPA. A parking ticket. Two tinfoil chocolate wrappers. I smell the armpits and gag. His BO is as potent as ever.

I see a box of books in the corner, next to a mostly empty shelf. That box is how I will be able to ID him. I know his book collection. All that's out on the shelf is *Moby-Dick*, one of his favorites, and a copy of *The Lord of the Rings*, out of character. I frantically step over a few boxes and trip into a pile of laundry, falling on my knees right in front of the book box. I puncture it with my keys and rip at the tape. I reach in, knowing I could find an inscribed book in there, since I know which ones I or other women have written in. I memorized all the inscriptions.

But then I hear the fumbling of keys in the door. Blood rushes to my head and my eyes momentarily black out, I could be concussed—but I breathe and steady myself with a hand against the wall. *No, no, no, no, no. We're not doing this.* I can't have him find me in his fucking house. Not here, not anywhere.

The front door opens and closes and I want to die right now. I wish a celestial force could mercifully still my heart and disappear my body. I get down to the ground and crouch behind the far side of the bed and box spring, curling up in the shape of an egg. There's rustling—sounds like plastic bags, the clunk of items, groceries. A chair moves, scraping against the floor. Then it's quiet.

I have to get out the window, it's the only possible way out. I rise up to all fours and I reach for the window ledge near his bed, but he must have heard me, he must have sensed a presence, because he yells out, "Hello?" And there it is. His voice.

I hear footsteps coming down the hall. I drop back down and become a rock again. My chest gets tighter. I scrunch up my face. Like it might keep him from recognizing me. I could text someone to help me. I could take his bedside lamp, run at him, and nail him on the head.

He pauses. He doesn't come closer. He goes past his bedroom, thank god. He moves down the hall, mumbling faintly as he walks. Then he stops again. A silence follows that feels long. I bet he can hear me breathing. Maybe he's got a wild smile on his face because he's got me where he wanted me all along. It takes everything I have not to lift my head to try to get a better look, not to stand up and say, *Fuck it, take me, I'm here.*

But the footsteps start again. He continues down the hall. I hear a door open, the creak of a twisting old knob. The shower goes on. This is my chance.

I shoot up, shove open the window next to his bed, one-two punch the screen out of the frame, and scramble my legs over the ledge, landing in a bush but immediately propelling myself out of it, somehow, onto my feet. I gulp the air with stout piglet wheezes and immediately, stupidly, I run over to his car again. On impulse, like it calls to me. And so it did, because, there. There. There. There it is. My smoking fucking gun. The sweatshirt is gone off the front seat but the book is still there—and now I can see the cover. *Listen Harder: The Erotics of Psychotherapy.* The book I gave him.

Rage and delight. Grief, dread. The night has grown a few shades blacker. I cover my hands with my sweatshirt sleeves, spot and rush toward a hammer on a small hanger of tools in front of where the farthest car is parked, take it, and with a mild running start, smash P.T.'s passenger-side window, until all the safety glass has fallen like cubed snowflakes. I slam and crack the back passenger window once, too, for good measure, then toss the hammer at the hood of the car, denting it. As I do I say out loud, to the dark, to him, because god knows he could be listening, "Leave me alone, you son of a bitch!" I reach in, take the book on the front seat, and then run like hell back to my car, lit up, fueled. Every cell waiting to hear him behind me.

I sleep with the light on when I get home, after a drive that took me twenty-five minutes longer than it should have because I drove far past my street without noticing. Actually, I don't sleep, despite three trazodone. I sit. Waiting, I guess, for him. He's got to know it was me. For all I know, he videotaped the whole thing. He brought me where he wanted me, and I did the thing he wanted. We could do this dance forever.

Outside, across the courtyard, the view from my bed, I see rainbow Christmas lights strung in the windows of a few of the apartments. Blinking in a nonsensical pattern. I can't imagine ever having the gumption or energy to put up holiday decorations.

22

It's 5 p.m. when I arrive at Afterlife. It's been three days since the break-in, and this is the first time I've left my apartment. No word from him yet, and nothing has been left at my door. It's almost Christmas. Fewer cars on the road and one of those winter days it's raining in LA. I have no umbrella so my hair is soaked, as are my sneakers. Code Red is sitting on the edge of the bar looking at her phone, a damp rag curled up like a little cat on her thigh. She's loudly listening to depressing pop ballads, and I'm pretty sure, as I stand in the doorway, I see her wipe a tear away. She's in a tan hoodie, HOKAs; her nails look fresh. I slide onto a stool and without looking up she yells, "I love you, I honor you, but we aren't serving for another two hours."

Her face transforms from exasperation to extreme confusion when she sees me. She reaches over and turns the volume down.

"It's you again, Jesus. Are you stalking me?" She lets out a little laugh, but I can tell she's uneasy.

"Uh, well . . ." I don't answer that. "Listen. This will be the last time, okay? I just wanted to let you know something. The guy I asked about? He *was* my boyfriend at one point."

She looks at me, clenches her fist, twists her face. "I knew it," she says, spinning around and hopping off the bar. "No one sniffs around looking for old classmates. You don't have social media? Please."

"Well, I only have a finsta," I say.

"But you know what? I get freaks in here all the time, and you just gotta swoop down to y'all's reality, and I thought maybe, sure, this weird woman just wanted to find out if I was fucking some guy she went to school with or whatever."

"Sure. Fair."

"And what? What do you want to tell me? You're still fucking?" She takes some well vodka from beneath the bar and fills up a shot. She lifts it to me, then gulps it. Her energy reads mentally unstable—but who am I to judge? Her eyes water from the sting. She pours another and shoves it toward me, unpleasantly. I take it with no protest or thanks.

"No, we are not," I say, my eyes watering, clearing the searing burn in my throat. "When we dated—wow, that's some brutal juice—I, uh, I really thought he was the second coming. But to be blunt, he's nuts. And he sucks. Like to the point where, I'm sorry, he really is a little, or a lot, dange—" Code Red starts to cry, her face turning the color of a ripe berry.

"Wait, no." I wave my hands at her like that will help her stop crying. "Oh, god, I'm sorry. I'm trying to warn you—"

"No need!" she says, kicking something I can't see but that sounds like a metal trash can. "He dumped me! Or whatever the hell you call rejecting someone you aren't actually dating!"

I try to open my mouth to apologize but she continues. "But like, yeah! Hope you're both happy! We're fucking and sexting all the time over the course of like, almost two months? And the whole time, he won't leave me alone, texts, songs in the middle of the night, constantly asking for nudes. Then we get into this weird fight the other night when he was over, basically because he got embarrassed that he went soft when I asked him to stick it in instead of eat me out. So he left in a huff, and said, as he left me ass-naked on my bed, 'Just so you know, I'm fucking other people.' "

"Well, I want to tell you something, okay?" I interject. "You are lucky it ended quickly. Trust me. I should have told you earlier than I did, but I dated him for a little over a year and he harassed me when we broke up. Hard-core. Some stalking. I couldn't even tell if he liked me for most of our relationship—then I had to get a restraining order."

She wipes a tear with her shoulder, then again with the bar rag. So gross, I can't help but think it.

"Oh god," she says. "That's insane."

"It was bad, yeah."

"Great," she says. "So, he's a crazy person. I'm devastated even when a lunatic discards me. Like usual."

"That's not uncommon," I say, suddenly feeling like I, too, am going to cry. I look down at my damp sneakers. "And I should have told you the first time we talked."

"It's okay," she says, then adds, "Actually, no, it's fucked. And that you asked me all that stuff. You didn't think it was important to say something?"

"Yeah, I know, I know, I know," I say. "And are you sure you're totally broken up? Like he knows that, too?"

"Oh, he instigated it after the fight. He texted me yesterday and said, 'Don't call me anymore, I know you're the one who fucked up my car.' Like, what? And then blocks me a few minutes later, after I told him repeatedly I didn't do anything to anyone's car. I don't even think something happened to his car, to be fucking honest. I think he was saying that as some bullshit lie, but whatever."

"What did he, uh, say happened to his car?" I ask slowly. I take a seat at one of the stools and place my hands on the clammy wooden bar edge to steady myself.

"He *says* someone smashed the windows of his car. If it's even true, it was obviously some addict or something, because it's LA. But he thinks it's me? And I'm like, for what reason? Because he's embarrassed he went soft?"

I nod, unsure of when to interrupt.

"My car has been broken into like four times. But there's not, like, a camera to prove my innocence. Again, even if it is true. I fully believe he's using it as an excuse to ghost me."

"Did he go to the police or anything?" I wonder if she can see that the corner of my mouth is twitching.

"I don't know. I doubt it. I mean, no one has contacted me, so . . ."

I let out a massive sigh of relief. Code Red cocks her head at me, just slightly. I catch my reflection in the mirror behind the bar, my hair stuck to my head and two shades darker from the rain. Mascara racoon eyes. A cut-and-bruise duo still on my left cheek. It all exacerbates the graying pallor of my complexion. Holiday lights, because they're everywhere now, framing the booze, a tiny luminous rainbow. Twinkling on my skin. I look as I feel. Deranged.

"So, you think he's . . . not going to press charges?" I ask again, after a moment.

"I didn't do it!" she yells. "Damn!"

"Right, obviously," I say.

"You think I did it, don't you?"

"I really, truly don't," I say.

"His insurance is covering it anyway, so it doesn't fucking matter." She blows her nose into a napkin with the Jameson logo printed on it. It seems very out of character that P.T. would have insurance. But he's been surprising me this whole time, I guess.

"So he thought it was you because he told you he was sleeping with other people?"

"Yeah, I guess," she says. "Plus, the only thing missing from the car was this book I gave him after our first night together. Some pretentious bullshit my ex gave me." She gave him that book? I lift entirely out of my body, hover a few inches above and to the left. Is it possible that two women gave him the same book? I half listen for a while to her complaints, nodding, then answer a few more questions about what he was actually like. Horrible, I promise her.

"He's done a real number on me as you can see," I tell her. She nods with a tight-lipped smile, and we very awkwardly shake hands.

It's only when I'm pulling into my apartment lot that I realize—I didn't ask if she had figured out his name.

23

At the mailboxes, by the entrance of my place, Courtney is wearing a Santa hat and sliding a little red envelope into each box. I'm dragging my embarrassing roller backpack down the hall, the wheels sounding like a pack of drones on the old wood. It's Christmas Day, and I'm on my way to my mother's for the wedding. Of course she made a stink that I didn't come for Christmas Eve, but the ticket was only $200 if I left on the holiday.

"Oh my god, merry Christmas!" Courtney says when she spots me. She holds up a few envelopes and shakes them. "These are not from me, okay, they're coupons to Shakey's from the landlord. I would never."

I lean on the handle of my suitcase. "Coupons. Not even gift certificates. These guys!"

"Oh my god, right? It's giving Scrooge," she says, shoving the last envelope into a mailbox and turning toward me. "Where are you headed?"

"Ah, my mom's. In upstate New York. She's getting married on New Year's Day, so . . . I've been cornered into a rather long visit."

"My parents are in Pasadena, so like, I'm always cornered."

"Rough," I say, giving her a small salute, then think to ask, "Any word on our favorite runaway in the building?"

"Nothing, no." She lowers her voice and gently jerks her

head toward the hall to remind me Screaming Bird Guy isn't far. "I don't think they've found her yet."

"I'm going to take that as a victory," I say in a raised whisper as I begin rolling my suitcase toward the door. Just as I heave it over the threshold, however, Courtney calls me back with a gasp.

"Oh, wait! I forgot!" Courtney takes her Santa hat off and grips it over her stomach, like she's about to deliver the news of a soldier's death. "Maybe this isn't the time to bring it up, exactly, but I figured out who was putting shit at your door." I let go of my suitcase at the door and slowly walk back toward her.

"I was going to text you but I forgot, and like, the whole stabbing happened, and yeah, really, I honestly totally forgot. I actually saw it happen the day after that incident. I caught them in the act."

"You saw him?" I say, coming toward her body so suddenly she takes a step back. "Like could you make out his face?"

"Oh, yeah, but, I mean, it's a *her.*" She lowers her voice again. "It's that fucking asshole who lives in the basement? Below you? Which I should have known, because there was a point where she was leaving weird love notes for the woman with all the snakes, and when the snake lady rebuffed her advances it was a whole thing. There was spray paint involved."

"I thought it was a man who lived in that apartment."

"As far as I know, she's a woman. Their name is Marie, anyway."

"You didn't think to mention that? About the notes for the snake woman?"

"Again, I'm sorry, weird stuff happens here all the time. I didn't connect."

"So I'm her new love interest?"

"Um, no, not that. She gave some random reasons."

"Like?"

"When I saw her, she bolted back downstairs. So, I followed her down there and knocked on her door—she wouldn't answer but she did scream something about your loud shoes, and the fact that you don't get your mail regularly, so it spills out onto the floor in front of her mailbox. Then remember when your toilet flooded?"

"That's it?" I crane my neck forward. "She thinks I'm loud? And blames me for my toilet problem?"

"Well, no, her big complaint—and she came closer to the door to explain this one—it's that you don't put your trash and recycling in the right place, so she switches it? And one time, I guess, as she was switching the bags to the right dumpster, she slipped and fractured her wrist? And she knew it was you because there was a piece of mail inside. Your 'menacing mail,' she called it."

"You're kidding."

"I'm not. And like, what she did, it's harassment, honestly, so you could file a thing, and so could the building. But you wouldn't believe the rights tenants have, so it's going to take a while. I'm sure we could get you a discount next month, if that's of any interest," she says.

"You know, I think it might actually be about time for me to find a new place," I say, not knowing what to make of this information at all.

"Go with God, girl," Courtney says, and slowly I turn, bumping my suitcase down the stairs to my taxi, as she adds, "But you do need to put the trash in the correct bins, yeah?"

24

The wedding is beautiful, honestly. The inn is nice despite the neo-Roman theme. Since it's New Year's Day, all the garlands, flameless candles, and a glittery Christmas tree are still up. Mitch knows the lady who owns the flower shop, and she owed him a favor, so there are massive bunches of cream, peach, red, and orange roses and wreaths of poinsettias all over the place. It's all so kitsch it reads as purposefully camp. It's a lot, but that seems better than a little.

It snows just as we sit down for dinner, the sky an ecstatic, celebratory pink. The wedding is bigger than I expected. Tons of people from town, my mom's friends and her coworkers from her last job, a few friends she's kept from the city, Mitch's massive extended family, and his delightfully frightening motley crew of employees from the lumberyard. On our side, bloodwise, just me, Mom, and Damian. I give a little toast and read a poem, our tradition. This time it's "Epithalamium" by Louise Gluck.

There were others; their bodies
were a preparation.
I have come to see it as that.

Maybe a little on the nose. The youngest of Mitch's *nine* brothers then sings an original country song he wrote for the occasion. He's wearing a denim suit coat.

At dinner I'm sat next to Damian on one side, who is flirting with the date he brought, and on the other, a guy in adult braces who does the books at Mitch's business. Eventually our conversation leads us to the revelation that we're both on the same mood stabilizer.

"I feel so understood," he whispers. After a few whiskeys I watch his face turn into a sad-clown mask as he tells me I look like his wife—who is currently home with strep throat—when she was younger. Damian apparently hears him say that even while talking to someone else, because he reaches over without looking at me and squeezes my thigh.

Just before dessert my mom takes my hand and leads me from my seat through the back door of the dining room, up the stairs of the inn, to the room where we got her ready earlier. Following behind her reminds me of being a child, the way she used to grab me sometimes when she was excited and wanted to show me something. A fox in the yard or a piece of art she'd made as a kid and found in a box, a song she was listening to she was sure I would like. Those moments gave her frequent bouts of emotional absence all the greater sting—the fact that she could light a person up like that. More often than not, as an adult, I focus on how I feel wronged by her, which is childish. I still hate that she could pull me into her lap while we watched a movie, lovingly scratch my head until I dozed off, then moments later shut the door to talk to some rando on the phone during our bedtime routine. Announce Damian would be making dinner—Ellio's pizza, until he taught himself, quite proficiently, to cook—because she was going out to a folk concert with Ben the traveling sales rep from work, she thought she had mentioned it, she was sure of it. Leave for drinks with the girls, crying, because some guy she was Hotmailing had disappointed her. And there I'd be left, confused, like, *Wait, wasn't it you a mere few hours ago who held my hand as if it were a warm egg and your palms a nest anticipating the arrival of life?* When I first met Bunny she reminded me of my mother a little, in the sense that she was able to be so profoundly present at times, to make you feel held with even the briefest contact. But Bunny has always been more capable of sustaining that care. My mother only makes you aware it's possible. When I was a teenager I thought she was an idiot because of how obviously her capacity for happiness was controlled by men. I resolutely determined I would never let a lover rule my life, and later on, when I did, I hated her more for my inheriting her disposition.

"What's up, Mom?" I stop at the door frame. Hesitant to come all the way in. I notice there is mistletoe hanging above me.

"I need your help, babe, fixing my hair," she says. "I'm so jazzed I don't think I'll do a good job."

She sits down at the vanity on the far side of the room, a marble-topped antique with a gilded mirror, atop which sits a creepy little cherub with perfectly round eyes. Right beside it is a window that overlooks the backyard, the twinkling outdoor lights lending a glow to the snow.

The surface of the vanity is covered in curlers, lip kits, and eye shadow. I know for a fact she recently found out about makeup tutorials on YouTube. She likes to "keep current." She would never let anyone else do her makeup because modeling and theater taught her to do it like a professional would. I got some lessons from her myself, very young, which I totally loved—how to do your eyes so they seem maximum wide, how to contour cheekbones. She taught me how to do her hair. Technically mine, too, but it's rare I put the instruction into practice anymore.

Her spine is straight, eyes spilling joy, waiting for me. She looks so much like a child. Her thick silver hair is in a mid-length braid—it's more flattering than when she used to dye it. She wears a very small, arched crown headpiece filled in with small flowers and gems and secured by copious amounts of hidden bobby pins.

She reaches into the calfskin Celine tote Mitch gave her for her birthday—something she has sent me multiple pictures of from all sides—and hands me her Japanese boxwood brush. Even when we were completely broke, she would order these brushes from Japan for the both of us, admittedly beautiful and well crafted, something she encountered on a photo shoot in Tokyo in the '70s. She credits them with maintaining the health of her hair.

She takes an open bottle of Pinot Grigio from below the vanity and starts pouring it into the glass she brought, then hands me the bottle—I take a swig. This prototypical wedding scene is not lost on me—brushing the hair of the bride—nor is the psychodynamic role reversal. Always the bridesmaid. To my mom. She prepares with such hungry delight, as though it's never happened before, each previous ceremony simply a dress rehearsal. Enthusiasm for weddings is confusing to me for this reason—it's meant to be such a deeply personal, particular expression of two people's love, yet most weddings are confoundingly the same. The celebration itself has a template, the vows have a script even when people write their own. It too often seems like an unexamined desire for sameness, an obligation, a necessity that keeps on keeping on despite its often amounting to something awful. It's no special take, a hateable opinion, but I can't believe most humans are meant to get married, built for it. Certainly fewer than those who do it. I get it can be a smart business arrangement, and people thirst for tradition, but if you're mostly going for love—well. You can, in fact, decide to stay with someone long-term, to make the choice to be with someone every day, without an audience or legal binding. Just as much as it's a vow of commitment to stay, it's a threat of bureaucratic misery if you choose to leave. We could find another way to get mutual tax breaks and have someone take us off life support, I'm sure of it. But over and over again, these proclamations of forever, these superlative descriptions of the beloved, these unequivocal absolutes. The fucking dresses. I read a statistic once that said there are about eighty-six divorces an hour. Still, I understand it's powerful to find a home in someone else, even for a little while, and marriage must seem like the most promising way to ensure you can keep it.

"Okay, what's the look you're aiming for?" I ask.

"Well, I thought I'd transition into something loose for the first dance. Preserve the waves from the braid with a crunch of pomade at the ends and a bit of hairspray, then take a bit from the front and twist them back and pin. My hair has been so thick ever since I've added biotin to my morning shakes."

"How do you come up with these things?" I ask, more in wonder than in judgment.

"Years of vanity." She theatrically bats her lashes. Even to this day it's hard to comprehend how her face was made. These large, frosty eyes, full brows, eyelashes that hit her brow bone. Her lips, upturned with such natural bounce it seems like invisible strings were placed at the edge of her upper lip, gently guiding them skyward. An aquiline nose with an even, softly structured tip. A long neck. Life has pulled on her features, but her beauty is stalwart and continues to announce itself.

"You've always been better about not caring too much," she says after a minute.

"I'm not sure if that is a compliment."

"Oh, for god's sakes, it is, Clarice. I wish I got my priorities straight much earlier on. Peace, serenity, savings accounts, all that jazz. And with men, too. I couldn't have been more off. I was into your dad because I saw him in an off-Broadway Pinter play and thought he looked like Andy Kaufman! We see how that turned out. You want someone to show up at the end of the day. Someone who buys you lunch."

"All's well that ends Mitch," I say. And then, abruptly, I add, "I think I saw P.T. a couple months ago."

"You did? Where?" For a moment we look directly at each other in the mirror.

"In a bar," I say, looking back down at the brush, rearranging the handle for grip in my clammy palm. I'm not totally sure why it came out so fast like that, other than wanting, on some level, to feel safer by saying it.

"Clarice, is he still bothering you? Following you?"

"I don't think so," I say, meaning it, finally. "I'm not totally sure it was him. But pretty sure. And it might have just been a coincidence."

"With a man like that, Clarice, honestly, you don't know."

"Obviously, I know that. But I've got no real evidence he even knows I'm in LA, and trust me, I've been looking for evidence. I think it was a fluke."

"So, you saw him and that was that?"

"Uh, well, I thought he was leaving stuff outside my door but it ended up being a disgruntled elderly person in my apartment building."

"You know, I've never understood why you wanted to live out there. I think that much sun absolutely bleaches people's brains, Clarice."

"That kind of thing could happen anywhere," I say. "Especially to me."

"Oh, don't be so hard on yourself. You've always been a little high-strung. Sensitive, I mean. That doesn't mean you're forsaken."

"From your lips to God's ears, Mom."

"If you stay open to it, you can find happiness, Clarice." She takes her hands and places them atop each other, then on her heart. I nod as I brush. "I'm serious, sweetheart, you've got to go on," she says. "You can live bigger. Live happily. If I'm nothing else, I'm proof of that."

There it is—always the same sentiment. She assures me I'm perfect right until the moment she tells me I'm making myself miserable. I have chosen a life of solitude, mired in self-pity. I am rigid and frigid. And I don't know—I guess it hurts so badly because she might be right. When I'm far away I think I'm free of feeling the well-trodden parameters of my mother's opinions, but near her, the space between feeling liberated and feeling lost gets blurred. I'm always the bitchy kid with her arms crossed, talking shit and ruining everyone's good time. Doesn't matter how old you get, I suppose; when your mom believes something different from what you believe, part of you believes you're wrong. And I know what my mom believes, she said so herself in her excessively long vows: union is the only real kind of freedom. I think maybe what she feels isn't freedom, it's relief—she has the dominant currency, committed external validation.

I exhale and look outside the window, hard. I spot Damian in his parka chatting as his date has a cigarette. He is eating a piece of spiced buttercream cake, which must mean he's a little buzzed. It's good; it's rare he allows himself anything sweeter than the sugar alcohols in his protein powder. Something is softening him, and instead of being happy for that, in this moment, I feel betrayed.

"My life isn't small, Mom," I say, making sure to keep my strokes steady. Looking back again at the two of us in the mirror, I notice my face is distorted and split where the edges of the three-paneled mirror meet. Before I left for New York, Bunny told me to be kind to myself, but also to go easy on my mom at the wedding, that her falling in love again is brave. I resent the idea that being a single person must be avoided at all costs, but ultimately, in spite of myself, I agree—falling in love is brave. Hope for something tender and unknown requires such nerve, it requires surrender. Unfurling your tightness. That could be, after all, what I lack. I am confused as to how my mother has that kind of courage and I do not, like only I caught a disease from a virus we were both exposed to. My mother, who has done about five minutes of self-examination, seems so much gutsier and healthier than me. More normal somehow, even when she's in the depths of self-delusion. It makes me feel like my attempts at intensive self-work are all for naught. I am not healing, I'm adrift. I am alone, which, to so many people, is the worst and weirdest thing you can be.

My phone—which during our brief makeover has been buried beneath bottles of hairspray, a curling iron, tubes of lipstick on the vanity—starts buzzing. As I unearth it I see, like bedeviling clockwork these days, it's my dad.

"See, Clarice, I told you," my mom says as she spots his name, the light in her eyes dimming ever so slightly. "He can sense when I'm in love."

We both watch the phone ring to voicemail, then she hands me some pomade.

"He's really sick," she says, her fingers curling into themselves where they lie gently on the table. "You know, it was him calling and breathing. I mentioned those prank calls to you? With the heavy breathing? It was him. His girlfriend caught him, then she called me. Humiliating for her, really. But I think he wants to say goodbye before he—you know."

"Oh, yeah. I guess I know. To be honest, I haven't decided if I want to talk to him before then," I say. When I open the smallest window into his life, it nearly kills me. "It might be better for me if I don't." I grab a pin on the vanity for the left side of her hair. We both notice at the same time my hand is shaking. She doesn't move to comfort me, she just looks down at her lap.

"Well, anyway, to answer everyone's questions, I guess he has a headset," she says, after a pause. At that I start laughing, and she does, too. I finish the left side, and she gives a nod of satisfaction while dabbing her eyes with a tissue. She gets up, drops her dress, steps out, and slides on a shift.

"I don't know if you will ever get over your fear of men," she says, right on target and out of nowhere. Her eyes are wine glassy now. "And I know I'm partially to blame."

"Why would you say that right now, Mom?" It falls out of my mouth. I can hear the soft catch in my voice; I'm ashamed of it. Just a second ago, we were laughing, at ease. "You think it feels good to hear that?"

She waits for a beat, confused, her gaiety suspended.

"Oh, come on, Clarice. I'd say it takes *much* more than that to hurt your feelings."

"It doesn't, actually."

"You have to do this right now?"

"Do I have to have feelings?" I scratch at the back of my head to ease the flood of emotion and walk closer to the window. I place my forehead against it, which feels so good and cool that I do the same with my cheek.

"What are you doing? You'll leave a smudge, not to mention wipe the concealer off that bruise you have," my mother says. Her dress rustles as she moves. "And you sound like a bad actress. Not everything needs to be dramatic."

"Thanks, Mom, for the compassion." My shoes suddenly feel much too tight. She sits down on the edge of the bed, which is covered in an unforgivable satin duvet, and pats the spot next to her.

"Listen to me, Clarice, I love you, and all I meant was that I feel, sometimes, that all of the men in my life had an impact on you."

"Right."

"I know things weren't always . . . right with those men. Even with your father."

"Yeah. They weren't always right," I say, sitting next to her.

I think I know what she means by that, but I don't think she's ready to actually say it, and I don't think I'm ready to hear it either. We might both combust if we went into the specifics.

"I didn't mean to offend you." She puts her hand on my back. "You've always been so self-conscious about being perceived. In any way at all. Good, bad, anything."

"It's not about being self-conscious. And, yeah, 'the men' did have an impact on me. And yeah, I care how you 'perceive' me, you're my mother. When you talk about my 'fear' so flippantly, it makes me feel like a depressing loser. I realize I've made three sets of air quotes."

"Oh, Clarice. A *loser*? What are you talking about?" She touches the tip of my chin. "I've said it before, you're a lot smarter than me. You made some mistakes, sure, but you're not—you didn't—I mean, you don't have children, for one. You aren't dragging anyone else around in the mud."

"Nope, just dragging myself."

"You can take care of yourself, Clarice, is the bottom line. You're not the type who needs someone else to do it for you. I always did."

"People are supposed to need things from each other," I say gruffly. She clicks her tongue. I'm being difficult. But she stands up in front of me and cups my face in her hands.

"You're very you, Clarice. In a way I never let myself be. And maybe that's a result of fear, or cynicism, or what have you. But it's made you very sturdy inside."

I nod and bite the interior of my cheek, trying, desperately, not to cry. My mom gives me three quick kisses on the forehead—something she used to do when I was a kid before putting me to sleep—then glides out of the room, back down the stairs, leaving me only the scent of her perfume. I curl up on that gauche bed, its headboard carved with even more cherubs, and let myself quietly cry for a while until I feel cleaned out.

As I lie there, this memory of my mom comes to me, from one weekend in high school; I must have been sixteen. It was very early in the morning, almost dawn. I was sort of half asleep, half in a weird dream—my mom and I were swimming with a bunch of teenage boys in a quarry. We were splashing around, having fun, but then we realized that the whole place was infested with snakes. I could feel them writhing around our bodies. I was so frightened in the dream that I fully woke myself up. I couldn't get back to sleep, so I read for a while, then went and made coffee around six. My mom is an early riser, so when she came into the kitchen, she was surprised to see me up. *Well, if it isn't Lazarus risen before noon!* She poured herself some coffee and sat in an armchair across from me, folding her legs underneath her like a foal. "I had a peculiar dream," she said, then went on to describe the exact same dream I'd had myself. Astounded, I told her about my own. It took me fifteen minutes to convince her I wasn't lying.

Two people so literally made of the same stuff, so connected on some cellular or spiritual level, that a dream could be passed between us the same night. Yet in real time she seems at an almost impossible distance. It takes years, such effort and restraint, to tell each other something like the truth.

25

My flight home is the day after the wedding—a red-eye—so I decide to ditch my broken suitcase for my high school backpack and go to the city early to hang out for a while. I get a cab to the East Village from the train, have some coffee, and wander. I walk west through dirty snow and intermittent freezing rain, get a cutlet sandwich at Faicco's, and continue up through Chelsea, up to K-town on Thirty-Fourth Street, then all the way back down to have a pleasantly disgusting glass of red at Sevilla. I think about calling Maxine to meet me but can't imagine updating her on my last few months, so I don't. She has a new partner, they're planning for a baby, things are different for her now. There's a glaze to the weather and a quiet in the air. It's January second and Christmas trees are in piles by trash cans all over the city. Such quick banishment in the name of forward motion. What's done is done, get on with it.

Living in New York always felt a little bit like doing a walking tour of the first part of childhood, and now, visiting, I can add the historical sites of my young adulthood as well. This is the health food store that Dad loved, the church where the Steiner arts summer camp was; that's where the video store, Alan's Alley, used to be, it's now a hardware store. There is the apartment on West Eighteenth I sublet for two months after college, and there lies the 16 Handles I puked outside of one time when I was drunk. On this bench I had a fight with P.T., during which, randomly, I got a bloody nose. This is where I had an interview for a job I didn't get. To be an assistant at a real estate brokerage? Something like that. Remembering it all is spooky but calming. It's nice to see this awesomely chaotic place, unmarked by me and my memories—instead perpetually created by every person who has ever passed through or stayed.

Around 8 p.m. I head down to the West Fourth stop to get on the A and head toward JFK. Normally, I'd spring for a car, but today I want to be in the crowd. I get down there and it's packed—it's a Saturday in the West Village, so people are starting to go out. New York is the only American city that likes the night as much as I do. This station has a particular scent, too, instantly recognizable. The smell of train fuel, and shoe soles wearing down concrete, every element of human body odor and the powerful wind of a fast train almost entirely clearing that odor, plastic, shit (rodent, human, dog), sat-on wood, smoke, dust and new clothes, trails of perfume, exercise, red-sauce takeout, sweet soft pork buns in a bag—no matter who you are, you have no control over the collection of smells once you're down here, you're powerless against it, no amount of money or prestige or planning could save you from breathing in the reality of this air.

The schedule says the express A is coming in about five minutes, but the local C is coming now. I turn to watch it arrive, momentarily consider, and decide against hopping on. I hear the announcement telling people to stand clear of the closing doors—and that's when I see him. Sitting in the middle of the train car, between a little kid and a man in a suit. He is wearing the same shirt he wore during one of the last manic episodes I witnessed—a night where he thought he had figured out how to restructure the US government. He's still chubby, his hair is short and close-cropped, and he's holding, of all uncharacteristic items, a Kindle. Then I see P.T. see me. His eyes bug ever so slightly. It does feel like time slows. Makes it possible in the span of seconds to take in all those details. The train jerks and starts moving, and I continue, mouth dropped open slightly, like a singing halibut on a wall, to stare. I shrug. I wave at him. Then I give him the finger.

I sit on the bench in the subway station while a few trains I could take to JFK pass me by. I still have plenty of time and I can't quite move yet. Gun to my temple, I can't decide what I feel. I send a few texts.

To Roz first.

It wasn't P.T. I saw, is all I say. *I'm positive now.*

I'll tell her more of the story later. Even the car window. She writes back.

I'm looking forward to processing this together. Happy New Year!

Then I text Bunny.

I'm glad he's not here!!!!

sorry I made u feel shitty about it

there's no doubt Ur power to manifest

Very real

Then Damian.

Wait, when did you think you saw P.T.?

You didn't tell me that.

You know you can talk to me, Clarice.

Then an email to Valentini.

I'm sorry, remind me who this is?

Then, finally, Rich, who, to his credit, does not respond.

Eventually an A arrives. Everyone on board is in their own world already, the way it should be on the subway, headphones on or chatting, paired off or in their small Saturday night groups, going out, swaying with the comfortable looseness of a few drinks. I can hear tinny music, from someone's earbuds, and next to me, two women are talking about an exercise class they resolve to take in the morning, even if they "go dark" tonight. They let out a little whoop after they say that, and I know they're talking about getting drunk, but I imagine the two of them, whose faces I can't really see, leaping into a gaping void together, a black hole in the middle of a clean sky, then returning, opalescent and gleaming, in time for interval training. It's not funny, but I'm deliriously tired, and something about the image hits me—I start laughing and feel an immediate pulse of self-consciousness when they pause for a moment. But they resume talking, and my shame dissipates, because who cares what I think, what they think—to them, I'm nobody. I put my sunglasses on and lean my head back on the window. I won't fall asleep in this brightness, knowing I have to get up again so soon, but my eyes close, they want rest, and my body is pulling at me, desperate to be still. I'll sleep soon. I'll sleep on the plane, I'll even buy a mask and earplugs at the airport news store, and when I get home, I'll get into bed, phone off, lights off, and sleep some more, with no end in sight, until I don't feel so tired. For the first time in a while I believe the world will let me rest.

Acknowledgments

Great thanks to the team at Knopf; my brilliant, whip-smart editor, Maris Dyer; and my agent, Eloy Bleifuss Prados, a truly wonderful, all-seeing old soul. Thank you to Joanna Lee and the team at Scribner UK, especially Ebruba Abel-Unokan, Ella Fox-Martens, Sophie Missing, and Imogen Bovill at Abner Stein.

For filling my life to the brim, and offering inspiration that in one way or another made it into this book . . . my many thanks to:

Mom, Marty, Conor, Ellen, Evie, Sam. Non, Mikey, Doug, Cindy, Caly, Caden. Maria, Jack, Maeve, Cath.

Natalie Sandy, Scotty Goldbeck, Chloe Tagliagambe, JJ Goldbeck, Matt Spelitch, Dove Ginsberg. Kiri Sulke, Philip Sulke, Nora MacLeod, Mika Bar-on-Nesher, Collin Frazier, Kara Clark.

Brion Vytlacil, Cara Budner, Elia Einhorn, Lexie Robinson, Stella Boonshoft, Valerie Fanarjian, Lisa Myers, Sydney Flint, Jude Dry,Nicki Ritchie, Rachel Joynes, Rebecca Sellon, Hope Smith, Megan Hill, Susanna Stahlmann, Rachel Katz, Lucy DeVito, Anastasia Simone, Rob Allen, Molly Greene, Lindsay Mancini. Sam Davis, Cyrus Gengras, Steve Marion, Matthew Vitemb, Stephen O'Reilly, Tom Lipinski, Mic Fingaz Daily. Gretchen Mattox, Russell Brown. Art Farm.

The New School, especially Alexandra Kleeman and Darcey Steinke.

420 Clinton 5B, The Lost Boys, Women in the Spirit, Fair Oaks Crew.

Lucas Kavner and Dylan Dawson, my first readers and guiding lights.

Sonny and Patch Darragh (thank you for reading my monologue that one night in the living room).

Dad, in his way.

A NOTE ABOUT THE AUTHOR

Annakeara Stinson is a writer whose work has appeared in *Bustle*, *Brooklyn Magazine*, *The Inquisitive Eater*, *IndieWire*, *Pitchfork*, *Marie Claire*, and more. She has an MFA in fiction from the New School and currently lives in Los Angeles.

A NOTE ON THE TYPE

This book was set in Janson, a typeface long thought to have been made by the Dutchman Anton Janson, who was a practicing typefounder in Leipzig during the years 1668–1687. However, it has been conclusively demonstrated that these types are actually the work of Nicholas Kis (1650–1702), a Hungarian, who most probably learned his trade from the master Dutch typefounder Dirk Voskens. The type is an excellent example of the influential and sturdy Dutch types that prevailed in England up to the time William Caslon (1692–1766) developed his own incomparable designs from them.

Typeset by Scribe,
Philadelphia, Pennsylvania

Designed by Casey Hampton